Robert Williams Buchanan

The Outcast

A Rhyme for the time

Robert Williams Buchanan

The Outcast
A Rhyme for the time

ISBN/EAN: 9783337271411

Printed in Europe, USA, Canada, Australia, Japan

Cover: Foto ©Andreas Hilbeck / pixelio.de

More available books at **www.hansebooks.com**

THE OUTCAST

A RHYME FOR THE TIME

ROBERT BUCHANAN

With Illustrations by

RUDOLF BLIND, PETER MACNAB, HUME NISBET, ETC

FIRST CHEAP EDITION

" Pœna gaudebis amara
Nominis invisi, tandemque fateŀere lœtus,
Nec surdum nec Teresiam quemquam esse Deorum."
—JUVENAL.

" There was a Ship, quoth he ! "
—COLERIDGE.

LONDON
ROBERT BUCHANAN
36, GERRARD STREET, SHAFTESBURY AVENUE, W.

CONTENTS.

*** The present volume contains the first of a series of poetic tales dealing with the Amours of Vanderdecken. The other tales will follow at intervals, until the series is completed.—R. B.

PREFACE.

"THE OUTCAST," issued to the public in 1891, was
the first of what I may describe as my "Satanic series,"
the most recent of which was "The Devil's Case." I
use the word "Satanic" to express the spirit of moral
and intellectual revolt, which is just as absolute in Vanderdecken as in the greater Devil. The same unrest and
unhappiness, the same dissatisfaction with the Divine
plan, the same appeal to Nature against God, emerge in
both characters; Vanderdecken, indeed, is the stormy
child of the Spirit of Pity. When the work is complete,
it may be discovered that neither the Devil nor his
favourite pupil has the last word, after all.

The critical reception of this work was, as usual, either
infantine or hypocritical; the popular notion of Poetry
being that it should be a sort of soothing syrup or nursery
rhyme, adapted to people who desire to doze out the little
span of life allotted to them. One valuable suggestion
came, among remarks truly appreciative and sympathetic,
from Mr. Herbert Spencer. Mr. Spencer suggested that
the poem might acquire additional variety, in the yet

unpublished portions, if the metres were changed more
frequently, and even the language of prose used upon
occasion.

A critic of the period has defined a classic as an old
book which is read by the young. " The Outcast " is not
yet an old book, but if the test suggested is applied to it,
it will be found to be already assuming classical preten-
sions. No work of mine, except " The Wandering Jew,"
has brought me so much correspondence from young
thinkers in all parts of the world, and I am constantly
urged to complete the plan, a somewhat exhaustive one,
as soon as possible. In answer to such correspondents,
I may explain that the work is well advanced towards
completion, and that I hope to issue it before long in a
definitive shape. In the meantime, the present volume
is perfectly complete in itself—*totus teres atque rotundus.*

ROBERT BUCHANAN.

July, 1896.

?

PROEM.

AD CARISSIMAM PUELLAM.

AD CARISSIMAM PUELLAM.

A GRAY Sea wrinkling dark,
And out on the dim sea-line
    A Barque
Becalm'd amid silver shine,

While gazing over the Sea
From an Isle of yellow sands,
    Sat we,
Holding a book in our hands !

Do you remember, Dear,
The time and the place and the tale ?
    The drear
Ocean, the one sad Sail ?

We sat there, spirit-stirred,
In the rainy Hebrides,
    And heard
The wash of the windless seas,

While ever, upraising eyes,
We saw the Ocean, the gray
    Cold Skies,
And the Sail afar away !

Still, as the still hours fled,
That day of gentle gloom,
    We read
Our tale of Death and Doom,—

Of the Outcast woe-begone
Who, mid the Tempest's roar,
　　　Drave on
Homeless for evermore.

Dearest, his piteous tale
Made your clear eyes grow dim ;
　　　Snow-pale
You read, and you pitied him !

" How sad, how strange," you sigh'd,
Out 'mid the Storms to roam,
　　　Denied
The lights of Heaven and Home !

" Dead, yet a thing with life,
Under the blight and the ban,
　　　At strife
With God, forgotten by Man !"

I whisper'd "Nay, but hear
How he learn'd the Love Divine !"
　　　More near
You crept, and your hand sought mine ;

Under those sunless skies,
We follow'd the dark strange theme,
　　　Our eyes
Alive with love and dream ;

And then, when the tale was done,
And you turn'd your face to me,
　　　The Sun
Shone out upon the Sea :

Rainy and dimly bright
Out of a cloudland pale,
    The Light
Stream'd on that lonely Sail ! . . .

We thought of Poets lost
Whose souls still voyage on,
    Storm-tost
By His wind, Euroclydon ;

Born to divine despairs,
Kingly yet trampled down,
    Sad heirs
Of the Martyr's cross and crown.

We thought of the English-born
Childe with the bleeding breast,
    All scorn,
Pride, and sublime unrest.

Yea, and that other too,
Pallid and radiant-eyed,
    Who drew
The Hyperion glorified !

We thought of Singers dead
Who shared the Outcast's doom
    And shed
Songs on the Sea, his Tomb :

Of him who wildly flies
No more on the Waters deep,
    But lies
Iu gray Montmartre, asleep !

[How loud his shrill voice rang !
Yet often his voice grew clear
     And sang
Songs that a child might hear !]

Of him who strongly smote
The Scald's harp laurel-crown'd,
     Afloat
On a stormy Surge of Sound !

Softly upon my breast
I laid your golden head,
     And prest
My lips to your brow, and said :

" Mine was that Outcast's doom,—
Tost mid the surge of shame,
     All gloom
Until my Darling came !

" Scornful of Nature's plan
I nurst my pride and grief,
     A man
Stony in unbelief.

This little hand of snow
Touch'd the hard rock, my heart,
     And lo !
Its stone was cleft apart,—

Then came the blessed dew,
The consecrating tears !
     I knew
God's Love, after all those years !

" Thus was I saved, redeem'd,
As even His Outcasts are ! "
    Bright gleam'd
The Light on the seas afar !

We sat there, spirit-stirr'd,
In the rainy Hebrides,
    And heard
The wash of the windless seas,

While rainy and dimly bright
Out of its cloudland pale,
    The Light
Stream'd on that lonely Sail !

THE FIRST CHRISTMAS EVE.

THE FIRST CHRISTMAS EVE.

' A WORLD without a God !   Heigho ! . . .
The good old God had merit, though !
Le Bon Dieu, gravely interfering
   In all Humanity's affairs,
Bowing His kind gray head and hearing
   The orphan's moans, the widow's prayers,
Was worth, or so it seems to me,
Whole cataracts of Tendency ;
For though He now and then grew crusty,
And damn'd some few (as all gods must), He
Was patient 'spite deep provocation
With the small things of His creation !
Jesus He loved, and tolerated
   Even Goethe's patronising nod !
Century on century He waited
While great philosophers debated,
   Then, finding men dispense with " God,"
Took His departure from the earth,
   Where still some limbs were genuflected,
The day that Schopenhauer had birth,—
And left the human race dejected ! '

Without, while in my chambers dreary
   I mused and watch'd the flickering flame,

The snow fell thickly, night winds weary

Moaned *miserere ! miserere !*

And shivering revellers went and came.

'Twas Christmas Eve !   The bells were ringing

In faintly joyful jubilation :

I heard the tidings they were bringing

But groan'd apart in indignation.

My plans in life had all miscarried ;

My only friends were dead, or married ;

My book (that Epic you remember)

Had gone to wrap up cheese and butter ;

And lonely, in the lone December,

As feebly as a leaf may flutter

From bough to bough while bleak winds blow,

Till rough feet tread it in the mire,

This heart of mine had sunken low,

Dead to the world and its desire !

' Confound their superstitious revels !'

I murmur'd, spirit-sick and sour,

' I'll dine with Care and the blue devils

And curse the world with Schopenhauer !

There is no God, and all men know it

Except the preacher and the poet ;

Women are slaves and men are flunkeys,

The best but well-developed monkeys,

And Virtue is—a huswive's sampler,

Self-sacrifice—an usurer's chatter ;

Once Heaven was sure and Hope was ampler,

But now the Devil rules Mind and Matter !
Le Roi est mort—destroy'd and undone,
Or impotent and deaf and blind—
So *vive le Roi* of Hell and London,
Who weaves a shroud for Humankind ! '

Peace upon earth ! goodwill to men !
The bells rang out with sad vibrations.
I poked the fire, pursued again
My misanthropic meditations.

' The last new Philosophic Pill,
A panacea for every ill,
Is—' Quit thy service in the Shrine
Prophets and seers have deemed divine,
Give up the Sphynx's dark acrostic,
Be neither atheist nor agnostic,
But, since thy days are just a span,
Worship and praise the new God, MAN !
He shall endure when thou art dust,
Gain that of which thou art bereaven,
He shall absorb thy love and trust,
Thy dying struggles shall adjust
The ladder which He climbs to heaven !
The better thou, the grander He,
This god of thee and thine, shall be !
And in the thought of His perfection,
To which all creatures are proceeding,

Thy soul shall 'scape from its dejection
  Caused by too much eclectic reading!'
Service of Man,—or Monkey?   Far
Better to sit rectangular,
And like a dervish contemplate
  My very navel till it grows
The central whirligig of Fate,
  The Rose of Heaven that burns and blows!
Better to dance with barefoot souls,
Like good John Calvin, on hot coals,
And, full of sin yet grace-deserving,
Face the Arch-enemy without swerving!
But worship MAN?   Go back once more
To image-worship as of yore,
And bend my head and bow my knee
To this King Ape, Humanity?
This stomach-troubled, squirming, aching,
  Mud-wallowing, creature of a day,
This criticising, this book-making,
  Fretful, dyspeptic, thing of clay!
This Multi-face whom it hath taken
  Ages to learn to wash and dress!
This horde of swine, doom'd to be bacon,
And now, by countless devils o'ertaken,
  Shrieking in impotent distress!
This mass of foulness and of folly
  Through whom the Paracletes have died!
This Yuletide carcase deck'd with holly

In honour of its Crucified !
Now great Jehovah lies o'erthrown,
Shall the mere Pigmy reign at last ?
Pshaw, rather worship stick or stone,
And let Humanity crawl past !

' Man as an individual, I
Hold first of creatures 'neath the sky,
But though I'm human at the best,
Man the Abstraction I detest !
Collectively, this Human Race,
Despite its brag and self-acclaim,
Its pride, its pompous talk, is base ;
Ever, in every clime and place,
Its record is of sin and shame !
Bright holocausts of martyr'd blood
Mark its progression up the ages ;
The sensual protoplasmic mud
Bespatters even its Seers and Sages !
Nay, what are all the human crew
But maggots from corruption bred ?—
' By heaven, we talk like gods, and do
Like dogs ! ' Nat Field has wisely said !

' A poor half-witted Caliban,
Wailing his nature and condition,
Still prone upon the mud, is Man,
And ne'er can be his own Magician ;

Far less, far less, his own supreme
    Master and Lord and Arbitrator !
Nay ! till the stars shall cease to gleam,
The wretch shall blunder in a dream
    And say his *Noster in cœlum Pater !*
In Heaven (or if you please, in Hell)
    Must reign the Lord of man and woman--
Not 'mid these shadows where we dwell;
Not on this blood-stain'd sward where fell
    The foolish gods who have loved the Human.
Nay, man can ne'er by man be shriven,
    By borrow'd rays his star must shine,
Not threefold heritage in Heaven
Could purge his spirit of its leaven,
    Or make the Upright Beast divine !'

. . . While thus I mused, I heard without
    A foot that blunder'd on the stair,
Then sounds of one who groped about
To find a door—'Some dun, no doubt !'
    I thought, not rising from my chair.
Then some one softly knock'd.   I stirred not,
But sat stone-still as if I heard not. . . .
Again !—' Come in,' at last I cried,
Whereon the door flew open wide,
And on the threshold there was seen
A Stranger, elegant of mien,
Tall, white-shirt-fronted and dress-suited,

Faultlessly gloved and neatly booted,
Who, paletot upon his arm,
  Opera hat upon his head,
Smiled at my start of vague alarm,
  And pausing ere he enter'd, said—
' Pardon this call so unexpected.
  I sail from England, sir, to-morrow,
And to your room have been directed
  A little kind advice to borrow.
If I have been instructed rightly
  You are a Poet, and the man
I seek for ' (here he bow'd politely),—
  ' I'm sure you'll help me if you can.'
So saying, he closed the door behind him,
  And threw his coat upon a chair,
While I, a little piqued to find him
  So confident and debonair,
Cried, ' Who the Devil are *you* ? '

                                    The light
Fell on his features waxen white,
His raven ringlets thinly threaded
With silver as he stood bareheaded,
His black moustache, and underneath
Two pearl-white rows of smiling teeth.
' The Devil ? ' he cried.   ' Pray, did you mention
That very primitive invention,
Who surely, whatsoe'er cognomen
  You give him—Satan, Ahrimanes,

B

Baal, Moloch—though he awes old women,
   The merest fiction of the brain is?
The Poets have invented for us
Some six or seven Fiends that bore us—
Chiefly the one your gentle Milton
Set the high buskin and the stilt on,
And taught to make speech after speech to
A God extremely given to preach, too!
Nay, Goethe even, though well acquainted
With his infernal subject, painted
A fiend impossibly malicious
And supernaturally vicious.
Sir, the real Devil, Science teaches,
Not only wears man's hat and breeches,
But shares Humanity's affliction.
In short, sir, Satan is a fiction,
Save in so far as we sad creatures
Assume his airs and ape his features

I listened in amaze, while he,
Smiling at my perplexity,
Advanced into the room and stood
   Full in the firelight's crimson glow,—
A lithe, tall form of flesh and blood,
   Yet pallid as the bloodless snow:
A modern shape such as we meet
   Cigar in mouth and homeward strolling
After the play, in Regent Street,

Where Phryne trips with loitering feet
And lissome Lais goes patrolling.

Answering his smile I cried, ' Who is it ?
Your name ? and why this midnight visit ?
Fixing on me his bright black eyes,
' A poet, sir, should recognise,'
He answer'd, ' one who has so long,
Been theme for satire and for song !
I' faith, I am somewhat widely famed
As PHILIP VANDERDECKEN, *named*
The FLYING DUTCHMAN ! '
      As he spake
I seemed to hear the surges break
On some steep shore, while thunder-crashes
Answer'd the Tempest's fiery flashes !
My head swam round—I shrank in dread
  From that world-famous Form of fiction.
' Pray calm yourself,' he laughing said,
  ' For we are fellows in affliction !
The cliques have damn'd *you* too, I hear,
For many a melancholy year,
Because, in trying hard to double,
Against a stream of tears and trouble,
The Cape of Desolate Endeavour,
And reach Fame's Ocean (smooth for ever !)
You used bad language, loudly swearing,
For great or small gods little caring,

You'd toss on Life's mad Sea until
You'd work'd your wild poetic will !
Sir, you lack'd reverence, as *I* did,
Who in my impotence derided
The Artificer of storm and thunder,
    The great Self-Critic of Creation;
And now, like me, you've learn'd your blunder,
    You hug your doom and desolation.
Well, well, let gods and critics be,
Sit down a little space with me,
Comparing notes, our friends commending,
    Cursing our foes, this wintry night !
Come, though our strife is never ending,
    We've had our pleasure in the fight ?
Not fearing Hell or hoping Heaven,
    We face the Elemental Flood ;
Far better to be tempest-driven
    Than rot upon the harbour mud !'

' A ghost !'

            ' A man!'

                        ' A poet's theme, .
Woven of nightmare and of dream !'

' Nay, flesh and blood, sir—there's my hand
To prove it !'

            Laughing low, I took
His ring'd white hand in mine, and scanned

His marble features like a book.
No sun-brown'd, wind-blown face, but one
Strange to the shining of the sun,
And sicklied o'er with sad moonlight
Beneath its ringlets black as night;
So young, and yet so old !—so still,
   So callous and so coldly proud;
The eyes so bright, the cheeks as chill
   As some dead sleeper's in his shroud.
Gazing, I heard, beyond the sound
Of happy church-bells ringing round,
The murmur of the sleepless Sea
Stirring and breathing balefully,
While Argus-eyed and strangely fair
   The wintry Heaven, stooping low,
Laid softly on its stormy hair,
With sighs of blessing and of prayer,
   Thin tremulous finger-tips of snow !

Then cried I, wakening from a trance,
   That sad sea-music in my ear,
' Whoe'er thou art, whatever chance
   Brings thee this night, be welcome here !
Spectre or mortal, man or devil,
   Draw up thy chair and toast thy toes,
And while the world prepares for revel
   Tell o'er thy rosary of woes !
I, too, as thou hast aptly said,

Have had my share of castigation ;
I, too, with fretful, feverish tread
Have paced the decks of life, and shed
    My sullen curses on creation.
Sit, kindred spirit, let's together
    Rail at the stupid heavenly fiction ;
Come summer days or wintry weather,
    We brood apart in contradiction.
We know the world—there's nothing in it,
    Now gods and heroes have departed ;
Palsied and feeble, every minute
    It grows more melancholy-hearted.
The Creeds have withered one by one,—
    Frost-bitten roses in the garden ;
There's nothing left beneath the sun
    But lives that pass and hearts that harden.
Sit down, sit down, my gallant Rover,
    And tell me, in the name of wonder,
What brought thee down the Straits of Dover,
To this sad City shadow'd over
    With fog and vapour, mist and thunder ? '

Then smiling, comfortably seated
    In the warm firelight's flickering glare,
He told his tale as I entreated,
    With tranquil after-dinner air,—
Turning his talk aside each moment
For light contemporary comment,

That showed him apt in whatsoever
   Was taking place from here to Hades—
Most diabolically clever,
   And intimate with lords and ladies ;
Familiar with the latest news,
   The freshest novels of sensation,
Scandal of palaces or stews,
The last misconduct of the Muse
   With bards of naughty reputation ;
Well read in Science, verst extremely
   In current philosophic knowledge ;
As intimate with works unseemly
   As any Fellow of a college ;
In short, an intellectual Dandy,
With every art of culture handy—
Libertine, with a touch of passion,
   Callous, but sadder than he knew—
Sceptic of course, as is the fashion,
   Yet somewhat superstitious too ;—
For fiercely as his wit might strike
On God and gods and men alike,
His furtive glances as he spoke
Belied the open laugh and joke,
As if he fear'd, despite the sneer,
   Taught by a secret intuition,
The coming of some Shape of Fear,
   Or some celestial Apparition !

He told me of his doom, and how
Despairing he had roam'd till now
From land to land, from sea to sea,
    In his doom'd Ship upon the Ocean,
As bored as any soul could be,
    And soul-sick of the troublous motion.
His crime ?   The form of his offence
Against avenging Providence ?
He laugh'd, and told me.   ' Unbelief !
    Too much philosophy,' said he ;
' I laugh'd at all the gods—in chief
    The Æon who is One in Three !
Although a sailor of the main,
    I was a man of erudition,
And having logic in my brain
Saw syllogistically plain
    The blunder of His Proposition !
For this, sir, and for minor sins,
    Not unconnected with Eve's daughters,
He pull'd my ears and kick'd my shins,
    And drove me out upon the waters.'
' A contradiction—if you knew
God was not, could God punish you ? '
He laugh'd.   ' Precisely !   Many a man
Has argued so since Time began !
But know the cause of my disgrace,
    And with my argument agree :
I swore to the Old Fellow's face

"In his doom'd Ship upon the Ocean."—*Page* 24.

He was not, and He could not be!
His thunder answer'd; but I proved
  'Twas only phantom-drift and cloud—
The more the elements were moved
  Against me, more I laugh'd aloud!
Then some one interceded—'twas,
  As usual, one of Eve's dear sex!
And on a day it came to pass,
  Standing upon the slippery decks,
I heard that I from time to time
  Might cease upon the waves to dance.
" Father, he knew not of his crime,
  Give the poor devil another chance!"
" One chance—a dozen!"—answered He,
Whom I had proved could never be!
So said—so done! The Eternal Force,
  Law, Love, Power, God, whate'er you please
To name it, steered my sleepless course
  To land for intervals of ease;
And there, at the divine request
  Of her who deem'd me worth retrieving,
I roam'd about and did my best
  To grasp what millions die believing.
In vain! in vain! where'er I went,
  Folly and Death were all I found,
My upas-tree of discontent
  With dead sea fruit was rightly crown'd;
I found both men and women rotten,

I saw no joys but health and money,
Love was a fable long forgotten,
   While Lust, though sweet, was poison'd honey.
I knew all creeds, all superstitions,
   All gods that men and women rever.
I tried all customs and conditions,
Adopted every priest's petitions,
   And got the same old answer ever.
The answer ?   Your dyspeptic German
   Has given it—Death ! Annihilation !
So back to sea, half ghost, half merman,
Scorning the terrors that deter Man,
   I hasten'd, sick of all Creation !"

I listen'd wondering.   Thoughts as drear
Had haunted me for many a year,
And yet so phrased they seem'd to be
Accurst and full of blasphemy.
Into his face I look'd again
   And saw my soul's reflection there,—
Pallor of passion and of pain,
   Shadows of cruel, black despair :
A spirit poison'd through and through,
Yet hungering for the sun and dew ;
A nature warp'd and wild, yet fraught
With agonies of piteous thought ;
A soul predoom'd to Death and Hate,
   Yet eager to be saved and shriven —
A life so wholly desolate

It seem'd fierce irony of Fate
   To mock it with one glimpse of Heaven!

' A hundred years ago,' said he,
   ' Began my folly or my crime ;
Since then I've kept a Diary
   To pass away my idle time.
Just for a joke, 'tis written in
Mine own red blood, on parchment skin
(Best for the brine and wet), and here
Upon my heart for many a year
I've kept it.   Would you care to view it ? '
So saying, from his breast he drew it—
A book with many a finger-mark,
   And placed it in my hand—and while
I glanced across its pages dark,
   He prattled on with cynic smile.

' Like a young lady, truth to tell,
I've kept my cordiphonia well!
My thoughts, my careless meditations,
   Are all set down in these queer pages—
My bonnes fortunes and my flirtations,
Sketches of ladies of all nations—
   Tall, short, dark, fair, and of all ages !
There's matter there of strange variety,
   Strange retrospects of sport and scandal,
Which any journal of society
   Would roundly pay, methinks, to handle.

They are at your service, if you please
    To use them—prithee look them over—
Memoirs are now the mode, and these
    Are highly spiced, as you'll discover!
They prove at least that such a quest—
    To find true love and self-surrender,
Is but a foolish, idle jest!
I've roam'd the world from east to west,
    Found many kind, and some few tender,
But never one prepared to give
Her soul that he she loved might live,
And Death's last draught of hemlock take
For some poor damnèd devil's sake.
I'll grant you, Man were saved and proved
Immortal, could he thus be loved ;
But no! the seed of Eve our Mother
    Is capable of much, but never
Of wholly losing for another
    All stake in happiness for ever !
They'll love, and even accept damnation,
    So they but hold their man the surer,
But absolute obliteration
Of self for his soul's preservation,
    Demands diviner powers and purer.
I've tost the gauge to God, and cried :
" Prove such self-abnegation to me !
Find such a Soul—I'll stoop my pride,
Admit the justice I denied,

With which you torture and pursue me.
Assume one Angel possible,
And God is surely proved as well !
Admit one soul from Self set free,
You prove Man's Immortality.
The problem's fair ! As I'm a sinner,
The Old One finds it hard of proving ;
I hold myself an easy winner,
After a century of loving." '

' *Peace upon earth ! goodwill to men !* '
The bells rang out around the room,
Beyond the frosted window pane
The still snow waver'd through the gloom :
Hung on the wall above my head
A prickly branch of holly bled
Bright drop by drop—berry and thorn
Symbolic of that Christmas morn !
' Not one,' methought ; ' yes—One, who gave
His life that those might live who die !
Rabbi,' I cried, ' come from Thy grave,
To give this mocking voice the lie !'

He laugh'd.   ' My wager, sir, concern'd
The softer sex and not the other !
A million hearts like yours have turn'd
For comfort to our Elder Brother.
In vain ! He found, as we must find,

The baseness of all humankind,
And broke His gentle heart in proving
Sisters and brethren not *worth* loving !
He, too, in that consummate minute,
    As I have done, His God denied ;
He play'd for Heaven and fail'd to win it,
    Bow'd a despairing head, and died !'

E'en as he spake the bells peal'd loud
    In clearer, wilder jubilation ;
He listen'd, with his dark head bow'd,
    A little space in meditation,—
His face toward the fire, his soul
Black as the sullen flickering coal.
Suddenly, from the embers came
A tremulous blood-red hand of flame,
Touch'd him upon the forehead, lit
His gloomy cheek and crimson'd it
As if with fire from Hell ! . . . and still
    The white snow waver'd through the gloom ;
' *Peace unto men ! peace and goodwill !* '
    The bells, in mockery of his doom,
Rang loud and clear !
                    ' Enough,' he said,
' Our King of Doctrinaires is dead.
Once, I believe, one wintry night,
    Hundreds of years ago, He rose,
And blunder'd with His ghostly light

Across the drift, amidst the snows,
Forded the narrow seas and found
The Devil and Pope Joanna crown'd,
Set side by side beneath the dome
Of great St Peter's, there in Rome ;
Then, finding He too soon had risen,
   And was not wanted or expected,
Back to his resting-place and prison
   He hasten'd sleepy and dejected,
And laid him down, and closed his eyes—
There, dead as any stone, He lies !
Poor fellow ! he was disappointed,
   Like all your dreamers in the end ;
What God the Father left unjointed,
Shapeless and vile, no priest anointed,
   No seer, no doctrinaire, can mend.
Enough of Him, enough of folly !
   What use o'er fruitless dreams to ponder ?
Pull down your evergreen and holly,
   And hang the skull and crossbones yonder.
Sweeter than constant introspection
   The light afloat which rovers follow—
There's not a creed will bear reflection,
There's never a god escapes dissection,
   Not even Jesus or Apollo !
I know where man stands *now !*—I've studied
   Your last philosophies right through—
Found my poor intellect bemudded,

Grown sceptical and bitter-blooded,
  And curst the whole pragmatic crew.
'Sdeath, what a waste of time, to pore
On all such melancholy lore—
Only to find this world as silly,
  As puzzled, as in times long gone,
When grew from Christ's pure Hûleh-lily
  The prickly λόγος of St John!'

He paused, then added, ' All this season,
  During my residence among you,
I've search'd the poor stale scraps of reason
  The last Philosophers have flung you.
I've read through Comte, the Catechism,
(Half common sense, half crank and schism),
  And Harriett Martineau's synopsis ;
Puzzled through Littré's monstr'-informous
Encyclopædia enormous,
  Until my brain grew blank as Topsy's !
I've suck'd the bloodless books of Mill,
  As void of gall as any pigeon ;
I've swallow'd Congreve's patent pill
  To purge man's liver of Religion ;
I've tried my leisure to amuse
With Freddy Harrison's reviews ;
I've thumb'd the essays of John Morley,
So positive they made me poorly ;
Turning to follow with a smile

The tea-cup tempests of Carlyle,
I've been amazed at times to view
    The proselytes Tom fill'd with wonder—
Ruskin, half seraph and half shrew,
    And divers dealers in cheap thunder.
I've also, Heaven preserve me! read
    Daniel Deronda! which was worse
Than any doom a wretch may dread,
    Except, of course, pragmatic verse!
The *Leben Jesu,* Renan's *Vie,*
I also studied thoroughly;
    I vivisected cats with Lewes,
    I tortured gentle dogs with Ferrier,
Found out just what grimalkin's mew is,
    And how tails wag in pug and terrier,
But came, however close I sought,
No nearer to the riddle of Thought!
With Huxley's aid, now much in vogue,
    I made cheap Knowledge all my own,
And kissed, allured by Tyndall's brogue,
    The scientific Blarney-stone!
I talk'd with Bastian, who affirms
    Spontaneous generation proven,
And, prone with Darwin, watch'd the worms
    Wriggling—like live eels in an oven.
Then finally, in sheer despair,
    Burn'd deep with Scepticism's caustic,
Found Spencer staring at the air,

C

Crying " God knows if God is there ! "
And in a trice, became agnostic !

' In this most fashionable creed,
Which even he who runs may read,
I found an Open Sesame
To England's best society.
The great Arch-Priest of Canterbury
    Kindly invited me to dine,
And with the Bishops I made merry
    Over the walnuts and the wine ;
Found them agnostic to a man,
But doing all good fellows can
To make their crank old Ship, the Church,
Still staggering on with many a lurch,
Take in her sails and trim her anchor
Before the Storm swept down and sank her.
I met Matt Arnold at their table,
    Where no Dissenter hoped to be ;
Voting the Trinity a fable
I dived as deep as I was able
    Into the " Stream of Tendency ! "
Then floating on, in 'soul's distress,
Currents that swirl to righteousness,
Was bound, half drowning, to assever
" Poof ! further off from God than ever ! "

' About that time I met a girl
With raven hair and teeth of pearl,

And just one touch of rouge to veil
The *ennui* of a cheek too pale.
One evening, after we had sat
In the Lyceum, wondering at
The great tragedian wrapt in gloom
Of Hamlet's sable cloak and plume,
We, strolling down at midnight-tide
 To the Embankment, paused to see
The two stone Sphinxes, heavy-eyed,
Crouching together side by side
 And gazing at Eternity.
" Behold," I said, " the Mystic Ones
Who know the secret of the suns,
And coldly sit in contemplation
Of the dark riddle of Creation ! "
She laugh'd. " My dear, don't heed " (she said)
" Those rayless eyes---try mine instead !
Love's the one riddle worth the guessing,
Woman the one Sphinx worth caressing !
Don't mind those stony ancient Misses
 Who cannot feel and cannot see---
Quit things incapable of kisses,
 And take a hansom home with *me !* " '

While, diabolically sneering
 At every system, foul or fair,
He prattled on, I nodded, hearing
 The echo of mine own despair---

Indeed, the mocking voice I heard
　　Seem'd more within me than without:
Yea, every thought and every word
　　Chimed discord to my dread and doubt.
Fainter and fainter, as it seem'd,
　　Grew the strange ghostly Form of fancy,
Till, rubbing eyes as if I dream'd,
　　I cried, ' By heaven, 'tis necromancy!
Ghost, *alter ego*, dull delusion
Of sense and spirit in confusion,
Begone! avaunt! back to the Ocean
Of vague primordial emotion
From which you came!'　But as I spake
　　He rose, with eyes that flash'd like steel!
' Nay, shake your sleepy soul awake,'
　　He said, ' and know that I am real!
Yet now my period of probation
　　Ends for the present, and I go
Back to the watery desolation,
　　The cruel Ocean's ebb and flow—
Hark, hark, they call me!'　Tall and wild,   .
　　He panted quick as if for breath,
His pallid face no longer smiled,
　　His eyes grew sunken, dim with death,
And from the distance, through the swells
Of moaning wind and Yuletide bells,
A faint sound broke upon mine ears
　　Of ' Hillo, hillo—come away!'

Then laughter as of marineres
    Hoisting their anchor 'mid the spray;
Nay, more, I seem'd to catch the sound
    Of whistling cordage, flapping sail.
I gazed aghast—my head went round—
The house seem'd rocking 'neath the bound
    Of billows shrieking to the gale.
' Once more, once more,' he moaned aloud,
    ' Adrift, unpitied, lost in gloom,
As lonely as a thunder-cloud,
    I fly to face the blasts of doom !
No peace, no rest, on earth or heaven—
    No respite yet,' I heard him cry,
' Spirit of Pain, to be forgiven !
    To rest a little space, and die ! '

Then all my soul was strangely stirred
    To pity, and my eyes grew dim ;
And quietly, without a word,
    I stretch'd my hands out, blessing him !
But louder, clearer, through the dark,
    With, ' Hillo, hillo, come away ! '
Those voices from some phantom Barque
    Rang, while he trembled to obey ;
A moment more, he rose his height,
His eyes shot gleams of baleful light,
His hands were clench'd, and with a shriek
    Of mocking laughter, he return'd :

'I come ! I come !'   But lo, his cheek
    Grew frozen, and though his dark eyes burn'd
With wicked fire, his body grew
    Bent as with centuries of care,—
  Transform'd he shrank before my view,
    With snowy beard and sad grey hair !
Yea, e'en his raiment seem'd to change
To something ancient, quaint, and strange—
Rags blown with wind and torn with storm
That round a skeletonian form
Clung wild as weeds.   Ah ! then indeed
    I knew God's homeless Outcast, he
Who, poison'd with the Serpent's seed,
Can ne'er be purified or freed
    Till Death shall drink the mighty Sea !
I saw him for a moment thus,
Storm-beaten, old, and blasphemous,
All desolate and all forlorn,—-
    Then, while I pitied his despair,
The bells rang in the Christmas morn,
    And he had vanish'd into air ! . . .

That was in Yuletide '77.
    Ten winters later I again
Beheld beneath the sunless heaven,
    Pallid in ecstasy of pain,
That outcast Shape ; or did I only
    Dream, and behold him as I dream'd

No longer desolate and lonely
 But beauteous and at last redeem'd ?
Of that sublime transfiguration
 My later song, not this, must be—
Meantime I mark in meditation
His dreary voyage to salvation
 Across a sad and sleepless Sea.

Here follow, tuned to English tongue,
The Flights of Vanderdecken, sung
By one whose soul oft seems to share
His doom of darkness and despair.
Accept the songs, O Reader ! weft
Of that strange Book the Outcast left,
 Mingled with warp of modern fashion.
Telling the story of his quest,
His weary wanderings without rest,
 I seem to plumb mine own soul's passion !

Here, then, the Modern Spirit stands,
Holding within his ring'd white hands
The Book of Doubt, the Writ of Reason !
 While foolish women weep and wonder,
He ponders in and out of season
 And gropes from blunder on to blunder.
He needs no Devil to beguile him,
While wine and wantons lure and wile him ;
He needs no God to thunder o'er him,

While Nature spreads her storms before him.
This is the Modern—this is he
Who would, yet cannot, bend the knee!
Who would, yet cannot, be once more
    A child in the soft moonlight kneeling!
All creeds he knows, all wicked lore
    That puzzles thought and palsies feeling.
How shall he yonder heavens afar win
    In poor Spinoza's merry-go-round?
How shall he 'scape the apes of Darwin,
    Dark'ning what once was fairy ground?
How in this tearful world, tomb-paven,
Shall he find resting-place and haven?
How?   By the magic which of old
    Set yonder suns and planets spinning!
By that one warmth which ne'er grows cold,
By that one living Heart of gold
    Which throbs and throbb'd at Time's beginning!
By that which is, and still shall be,
In spite of all Philosophy!
From that we came, to that we go,
    By that alone we live and are—
Core of the Rose whose petals blow
    Beyond the farthest shining star!
Safe, despite Nature's cataclysm,
    Sure, though the suns should cease to shine,
Love burns and flames through Thought's abysm,
    Serene, mysterious, and divine!

One little word solves all creation,
  Abides when Death and Time have passed—
Damn'd by the genius of Negation,
  Man shall be saved by Love at last!

AD LECTOREM.

Herein lies a Mystery,
If you but knew it!
Peruse this strange History—
You'll never see thro' it,
Till Love learns your blunder
And comes to assist you:
When, smiling and weeping,
With heart wildly leaping,
You'll find, to your wonder,
God's Angels have kissed you!

GENTLE READER,
Read herein,
English'd and versified out of the Double Dutch,
THE STRANGE FLIGHTS
of
PHILIP VANDERDECKEN,
called the FLYING DUTCHMAN,
Being a Record of
His Amours in all climes and countries ;
His experiences of all complexions ;
HIS CONVERSATIONS
with the great Goethe, and other persons of reputation,
some still living ;
His curious and often improper REFLECTIONS *on*
MEN, MANNERS, *and* MORALS ;
with a full, true, and particular account of
HIS VARIOUS RELIGIOUS OPINIONS ;
The whole showing, in a series of
Startling Episodes,
How, having been
DAMNED,
By reading the philosophy of Spinoza,
He was finally
SAVED
By the Love of a Woman.

CANTO I.

MADONNA.

CANTO I.

MADONNA.

MORE than a hundred years have fled
Since Philip Vanderdecken read
Spinoza, and was damn'd . . . .
                            For days
He ponder'd in a dark amaze
The Demonstration Absolute
Mortal nor angel can confute,
Which proves the Eternal One must be
Divorced from Personality;
Establishes sans contradiction
The fact more terrible than fiction
Of the mysterious Substance shed
Through stone and tree, the quick and dead,
Suns and the glow-worm, bread and leaven,
    Sunlight and moonlight, Fool and Seer,
Earth-dung, the nebulæ of Heaven,
    Shakespere's calm smile and Arouet's sneer
And having ponder'd every cranny
O' the argument, not missing any,
The Captain, standing all forlorn
In his brave vessel off Cape Horn,

Swore with a mighty oath and round
Spinoza's argument was sound !
'Damn me for evermore,' said he,
'If any Personal God there be !
If there be any worth a straw
Stronger than primal Force and Law,
Why, let Him show his power and keep
Our vessel struggling on the Deep
For ever and for ever.'   Thus
This Mariner most impious
Call'd on the Spirit of Creation
To approve Himself—by his damnation !

Becalm'd on billows bright as brass
That slowly 'neath her keel did pass
But broke not, lay the lonely Barque
Scorch'd by the sunlight, stiff and stark.
From the high poop the Captain view'd
The sad and watery solitude.
Tall, lithe, and sinewy, marble pale
Despite the stings of many a gale,
With hair as ebon black as night,
Black eyes alive with ominous light,
    White teeth, and lips of lustrous red,
Rings on his fingers waxen white
    As frozen fingers of the dead ;
And though the garb that wrapt his form
Was rough and fit to face the storm,

" The ship, a Dutchman weather-beaten, .
Roll'd like a log."—*Page* 49.

And of a long-past fashion, he
Was dandified exceedingly;
His whole appearance, all would grant,
Byronically elegant !
Nor young nor old, but just the age
To cozen maidens not too sage,
And kindle thoughts and looks that burn
In dames of a romantic turn.
The ship, a Dutchman weather-beaten,
With wind-worn sails and decks wormeaten,
High poop, and for a figurehead
A Woman Form with arms outspread
Stript to the waist, and serpent hair
Falling upon her shoulders bare,
Roll'd like a log, and rose and fell
Groaning upon the molten swell.
His crew, a hideous band, were such men
As only can be found 'mong Dutchmen—
Squat, fat, red night-capp'd, hairy dogs,
Gruesome and guttural as hogs,
Yet ghostly, with lack-lustre eyes
Full of strange light and dark surmise;
Faces that could not *smile*, although
Their voices croak'd with laughter low,
As they crept feebly to and fro.
They all were scar'd as by a brand
Held in some cruel Demon's hand,
And show'd the trace of every sin

D

That blurs the soul or stains the skin.
Most were the very froth and scum
Of mortal mariners, but some
Were well-born rogues of education
Gone wrong through vice and dissipation.
The mate, the meanest rascal there,
A lean thin rogue with hoary hair,
Could quote a thousand sayings pat in
Sanscrit and Hebrew, Greek and Latin,
And by the metaphysicians show
That black was white and soot was snow;
For he, so arm'd with wicked knowledge,
Had been Professor of a College,
And occupied with reverend air
The moral-philosophic chair,
Till wine and women, which so few shun,
Had brought him down to destitution,
And he had been compell'd to gain
His bread upon the stormy main.

The ruffians shared their Captain's doom,
    But each to him was as a satyr;
They watch'd him, while with looks of gloom
    He ponder'd deep on Mind and Matter;
Clustering at the mast they stood
    Like hounds that feel their master nigh;
They knew the devil in his blood
    And fear'd the lightning of his eye—

Then broke to many a mutter'd curse
On him and all the Universe;
For well they knew by many a sign,
    Within them and without, that they
Were exiles from the Grace Divine
And doom'd to toss upon the brine,
    Branded and curst, and cast away!

Three days and nights the calm had lain
    Upon the seas with blistering rays,
Hot as a forge the suffering Main
    Lay throbbing, flashing back the blaze;
On gaping decks and sails that hung
    Like shrunken foliage dry to death,
The heaven sent down a serpent's tongue
    Of sunlight, and with fiery breath
The burning Skies, the scorching Sea,
Embraced each other lustfully.
But salamander-like, while all
    His seamen cursed the sultry weather,
The Captain paced with calm footfall
    The blistering decks for hours together.
Indifferent to the beams that fell
On his proud head like flames of Hell,
E'en thus he poised and weigh'd and sifted
    The Problem with Spinoza's aid;
But when his eyes at last were lifted
    And his decision at last was made,

Suddenly, with a troublous motion,
The sleeping waters of the Ocean
Awoke and moan'd! thick cloud and gloom
    Enwrapt the ship, and sudden thunder,
With blood-red gleams and sulphurous fume,
    Tore the great darken'd Deep asunder!
And, lo! like monsters fiery-eyed
The great waves rose on every side,
And shriek'd, tumultuously driven
Beneath the fiery scourge of Heaven.
'Hoho!' the Captain laughed, 'is this
    Your answer, O ye Elements!
The same old argument, I wis,
    To justify Divine intents!
Think you I quail because *you* grumble?
    Think you I change because you swear?
By heaven, the Universe shall crumble
    Before you cow me into prayer!
Away! away! I heed your screaming
No more than any teapot's steaming!
Roar yourself hoarse, ye slavish surges,
    In awe of what appals the creature!
Swallow the pill that twists and purges
    Your watery bowels, mother Nature!
I, son of man, being man at least,
    Can still preserve my self-respect here:
What churns you Elements to yeast,
What terrifies each mindless beast

Awes not the form that stands erect here !
Away ! away !—Hell and the Devil
Approve your dread, while *I* hold revel,
And, scornful of your protestation,
Laugh, lord and master of Creation ! '

Long nights and days, through gulfs of gloom,
    The ship accurst was fiercely driven—
Now swallow'd deep in ocean-spume,
    Now lifted like a straw to heaven—
Like some struck bird that ere it dies
Trials its wet wings and seeks to rise,
But flutters feebly down again
Smit by the lash of wind and rain.
Still on the decks the Captain clung,
Lick'd by the lightning's serpent-tongue ;
And still his cold defiant cry
Answer'd the threats of sea and sky.
But when the Seventh Day dawn'd, behold !
A thin pale Hand of fluttering gold
Stole thro' the clouds, and silently
Touch'd the wild bosom of the Sea,
So that it softly rose and fell
With tearful sob and windless swell ;
And gently on the waters lay
The silence of the Sabbath Day.

O gracious day of peace and calm !
    When, sweetly and supremely blest,

On the world's wounded heart falls balm
 And frankincense of perfect rest !
After Creation's storm and grief,
 After life's fever and life's woe,
One long deep breath of soft relief
 Eases all Nature's lasting woe !
The Sabbath of the Universe
 Abides, though gods and systems cease—
The human doom, the primal curse,
 Is hush'd to sacramental peace.
Now and for ever, comes the sign
 God giveth His belovëd sleep,
While music of some choir divine
 Steals softly in from Deep to Deep !
It touch'd the Outcast's weary brow,
 It calm'd his stormy soul's distress.
He had not fear'd God's wrath, but now
 He trembled at God's gentleness !
Standing in desolation there,
 He seem'd to hear from far away
Soft chimes that fill the Sabbath air
 When happy mortals flock to pray ;
And o'er green uplands he could see
A spire—Faith's finger—peacefully
Pointing to Heaven !—A moment thus
He linger'd, pale and tremulous,
Then through his heart again there stole
The pride that poisons sense and soul,

And from his brow he shook again
The benediction all may gain—
'A day of rest! A day of peace!'
　Perish the lie,' he fiercely said—
'Nay, not till Heaven and Earth shall cease,
　Till Death shall mingle quick and dead!
If God could rest, Man resteth never!
Storm is his portion now and ever—
He laughs that one day out of seven
Shall justify the frauds of Heaven!
Accept your Sabbath, winds and waves,
　Rest for a little from your sorrow,—
The cruel Hand that made ye slaves
　Shall lash your backs again to-morrow!
Man knows no Sabbath, no cessation
Of utter storm and tribulation!
Man stands erect, defiant, knowing
From Death he comes, is deathward going!
Man, first of things and last of blunders,
　The crown of Nature and her shame,
Stands firm, and neither prays nor wonders,
　Lord of the Tomb from which he came!'

Suddenly, as he spake, the Barque
　With mist and cloud was wrapt around,
But as between the dawn and dark
　Soft lights of sunrise with no sound
Part the dim twilight and reveal

The morning-star as bright as steel,
E'en so the mist was blown apart
Like dark leaves round a lily's heart,
And in the core thereof were seen
Still brightning shafts of golden sheen,
Dazzling his sight—yet dimly there
      He saw, or seem'd to see, a Form
With saffron robe and golden hair,
Walking with rosy feet all bare
      The Waters slumbering after storm !

A Maiden Shape, her sad blue eyes
Soft with the peace of Paradise,
She walk'd the waves ; in her white hand
Pure lilies of the Heavenly Land
Hung alabaster white, and all
The billows 'neath her soft footfall
Heaved glassy still, and round her head
      An aureole burnt of golden flame,
As nearer yet with radiant head,
      Fixing her eyes on his, she came !
Then as she paused upon the Sea,
Gazing upon him silently
With looks insufferably bright
      And gentle brows beatified,
He knew our Lady of the Light—
      Mary Madonna heavenly-eyed.

" He knew our Lady of the Light—
Mary Madonna heavenly-eyed."—*Page* 56.

How still it was! The clouds above
Paused quietly and did not move;
The waves lay down like lambs—the air
Was hush'd in sad suspense of prayer—
While coming closer with no sound
She hover'd pale and golden crown'd
And named his name! And even as one
  Who from dark dreams of night doth stir,
And fronts the shining of the sun
  With haggard eyes, he look'd on her!

But as he gazed his sense grew clear,
His dazzled brain shook off its fear,
And all his spirit fever-fraught
From agonies of cruel thought,
Rose up again in callous scorn—
  ' Vision or ghost, whate'er you be,
Welcome afloat this Sabbath morn,
  Bright shining Wonder of the Sea!
Methinks I seem to know,' he said,
  ' That face so fine, that form so fair,—
They hung in childhood o'er my bed,
And from the village altar shed
  Soft influence over folk at prayer.
And yet, I know, 'tis only fancy,
  Some bright delusion of the brain,
Poor Nature plays such necromancy
  To cheat our reason, all in vain.

I would each optical illusion
That sets poor mortals in confusion
Were beautiful and bright and pleasant
As that which haunts my sight at present !
Rose of a Maid, I bend in duty
Before thy miracle of beauty !
Speak, let me hear thee—if a spirit
    Is capable of conversation,
By Venus, I would gladly hear it
    'Mid these dull gulfs of desolation ? '

How still it was !— and could it be
A voice that answer'd, or the Sea
Just stirring softly in surcease
Of tempest into throbs of peace ?
Low as his own heart's beat, yet clear
And sweet, there stole upon his ear
An answer faint like Sabbath bells
Heard far away from leafy dells
Buried in leaves and haze, so still
And soft it only seems the thrill
Of silence through the summer air—
A sigh of rapture and of prayer !

MADONNA.

Child of the Storm, whose spirit knows
No reverence and no repose,

Who disbelievest God the Lord
And holdest Humankind abhorr'd,
Knowest thou Me ?

VANDERDECKEN.

Madonna, yes !
How oft thy radiant loveliness
Has shone upon me with soft eyes
In earthly picture-galleries !
By Raphael's and Murillo's brushes,
So skilled to catch thy lightest blushes,
By Tintoretto and the rest,
Thou'rt even fairer than I guess'd !

MADONNA.

Dost thou believe in God my Son ?

VANDERDECKEN.

A categoric question, one
Most difficult to answer rightly
And, at the same time, quite politely :
Frankly, Spinoza's text has showed
The impersonality of God ;

And for thy Son, well, I opine
No mortal man can be Divine,
Nor may a maid who takes a mate
Conceive yet be immaculate !

MADONNA.

Blasphemer !   Is there man or woman,
Or any shape divine or human,
Or any thing, save Death and Sin,
Thy wicked soul believeth in ?

VANDERDECKEN.

Madonna, no !   I grieve to tell
I question Heaven and smile at Hell,
Believe all human creatures are
Accurst in each particular,
Especially the sex of madam
Who gave the fruit to falling Adam !

MADONNA.

Christ help thee !   Hast thou never loved ?
Never known woman's love, or proved
The depth of faith that dwelleth in her ?

VANDERDECKEN.

Never, as sure as I'm a sinner !
I like the sex, 'neath sun and moon
Have found full many a *bonne fortune ;*
But that deep faith have never met.

MADONNA.

Yet woman's love might save thee yet !

VANDERDECKEN.

Madonna, how ?   Though now, I fear,
Past saving, I would gladly hear !

MADONNA.

Then listen !   By the charity
Of Him who loveth even thee,
By Him whose feet flash'd down on dust
Shall bruise the hydra heads of Lust,
By Him, my Son, who cannot rest
E'en in the Gardens of the Blest,
But ever listening strains His ears
To catch the sound of human tears,
From Him, who fain would kiss thy brow,
I offer thee redemption.

VANDERDECKEN.

How ?

MADONNA.

Thy doom it is to wildly beat
Without a home to rest thy feet,
Monster, yet featured like a man,
And lonely as Leviathan.
So far thy doom hath been fulfill'd
And found thee stubborn and self-will'd,
But now my Son shall suffer thee,
    One short year out of every ten,
To leave thy Ship upon the Sea
    And wander 'mong thy fellow-men.
There shalt thou seek (and mayst thou find!)
Some gentle shape of womankind,
Who in the end shall freely give
Her life to death that thou mayest live ;
Who loving thee, and thee alone,
Flesh of thy flesh, bone of thy bone,
Heart of thy heart, content to share
Thy loneliness and thy despair,
Shall from the fountains of her soul
Baptize thy brows and make thee whole.
Then, with that woman, hand in hand,
Shalt thou before the Master stand,

Saying, ' By her thy love hath sent,
Lord, I believe, and I repent ! '

VANDERDECKEN.

Madonna, this thy boon to me
Seems somewhat of a mockery !
Have I not proved, do I not know,
By long experience here below,
No woman, howsoever tender,
So capable of self-surrender ?
Love comes, love goes, and is the one
Sweet conquering thing beneath the sun,
But never have I seen or noted
One human creature so devoted
That I could say, ' Her soul is mine,
And God is good, and Love divine ! '
Spare me the respite, if you please,
And let me stop upon the seas.

MADONNA.

Not so ! The Lord, my Son, commands,
And thou shalt search through many lands,
Yea, search and search, though it should be
Through most forlorn Eternity.
Thy manhood, in immortal prime

Shall triumph over Death and Time,
Thy face into the very Tomb
Shall peer, yet keep its living bloom ;
Nature shall aid, from Earth's dark breast
Shalt thou take gold to aid thy quest.
Begin thy search whene'er thou wilt,
Pass on through clouds of sin and guilt,
Range every clime, search every nation,
Until thou light on thy salvation !

So saying, as a star grows bright,
Then flashes into sudden night,
She vanish'd ! and the sleeping Main
Awaken'd monster-like again,
Shook the loose brine from its fierce hair,
And shriek'd in tempest-toss'd despair,
Then crouching for a moment, roar'd
Before the Lightning's sudden sword,
Thrust thro' and thro' and thro' it, and then
Drawn flashing up to the heavens again !
With whistling shroud and thundering sail,
The Ship sped on before the gale,
The seamen lifting spectral faces
With ' Hillo ! hillo ! ' took their places,
And on the poop, while on they flew,
The Captain thunder'd to his crew.

From night to day, from day to night,

Through gulfs of gloom the ship took flight,
Until, although the bitter blast ·
    Shriek'd still, and the great waves made moan,
The troubled heavens grew clear at last,
And through the storm-mist drifting fast
    A cold wan Moon was wildly blown,
And on the surge-vex'd ocean ways
    Shed down her melancholy rays.
Then gazing southward through the night
    They saw, o'er seas that blackly roll'd,
A starry beal-fire blazing bright—
    The Southern Cross of glistening gold!

Suddenly, as they look'd thereon,
The blast fell still—the Storm had gone !
And though the waves, too sad for rest,
Still heaved as one tumultuous breast,
The wind grew faint and stirr'd like dim,
    Breath on a mirror o'er the Sea,
While near the heaving ocean-rim
    The great Cross crimson'd balefully !
Then while deep dread and dim eclipse
    Lay on the watery solitude,
And on the decks with soundless lips
    And awe-struck hearts the outcasts stood,
Out of the ghostly twilight stole
Great frozen Spectres from the Pole.

E

Silent and dim and marble pale,
Like ship on ship with frozen sail,
They crept from out the vaporous gloom,
    Each misted with its own cold breath,
And cluster'd round the Ship of Doom
    Like shrouded giant shapes of Death.

Still grew the Deep with scarce a stir—
    Still lay the Barque, while all around
The Bergs, like one vast Sepulchre,
    Closed in upon it with no sound !
Small as a shallop floating lone
Under great mountain-peaks of stone,
Seem'd the great Ship, while o'er it rose
Crag beyond crag of ice and snows !
And now the little light had fled,
Chill shadows fill'd the air with dread,
And on the cold decks kneeling dumb,
Thinking the end of all had come,
With haggard faces seam'd with tears
Gather'd the woe-worn marineres.
But in their midst, erect and tall,
    The Captain stood without emotion—
He whom God's wrath could ne'er appal
    Smiled at those Spectres of the Ocean.
Still unsubdued and undismay'd,
Calm and superior, he survey'd

"Shrouded giant shapes of Death."—*Page* 66.

The crumbling peaks of strange device,
  The threatening towers, the chasms dark,
The cruel silent walls of ice
  That closed and closed to crush the Barque !
And for a time his lips were seal'd,
  But when his soul found speech at last
His voice like thunder round him peal'd
  From chasm to chasm cold and vast !
' Welcome,' he cried, ' ye shapes of Death !
  Goats of the Goatherd throned on high !
Come, Phantoms born of God's cold breath,
  And crush the dust that longs to die !
Give him the *coup de grâce*, ye Slaves
  Of that blind Force he scorneth still.
Annihilate him as he craves,
  Ye Monsters, at your Master's will !
Yet, if the hour be not yet here,
Crouch down like dogs and disappear,
Fade, Phantoms, from his path, and creep
To pasture further on the Deep ! '

Thunder on thunder answer'd him !
The great Gulf heaved, the heavens grew dim,
And like to thunder-clouds storm-driven
Together, crashing rent and riven,
Totter'd those shapes of ice and snow,
As if an Earthquake rock'd below !
While toppling peaks and crumbling towers

Darken'd the air with frozen showers,
Shrieking and waving frosty wings
The Bergs replied like living things !
And smother'd 'neath the snows that fell
As thick as lava snows of Hell,
Lay the doom'd Ship upon its side,
   Beaten and bent, but undestroy'd,
While still its Captain's voice defied
   God and those Spectres of the Void.
' Judgment ! swift judgment and no shrift,'
   He cried, ' are all for which we yearn ;
This life that was a Monster's gift
   Back to the Giver we return ! '
But as he spake a forkèd track
Of windless waters ebon-black
Was rent between the frozen mass
Of mountains—that the Ship might pass !
And faintly feebly quivering,
A bird with trailing broken wing,
The Ship crept on !

          Then loud and clear
Above the thunders roaring near,
The Captain laugh'd ! ' On to Cape Horn—
We'll round the Cape at merry morn—
Up ! up ! hoist sail ! ' And at the word
The frozen crew at last were stirr'd,
And gazing round with spectral faces

With ' Hillo ! hillo ! ' took their places ;
And slowly, through the Shapes of Snow
That drew aside to let it go,
Crimson'd by brightening beams of day
The Ship of Death pursued its way.

CANTO II.

THE FIRST HAVEN.

(NATURA NATURANS.)

CANTO II.

THE FIRST HAVEN.

I.

Whom shall I dedicate this Book to ?
  (Each Canto needs a dedication.)
I want some briny Bard to look to
  For sympathy and inspiration !
The theme is primitive at present—
  Nature undrest, without her stays :
To Tennyson 'twould seem unpleasant—
  He blends no vine-leaves with his bays.
Scorning the flesh and all things hot,
  Will Morris wanders *sans culotte*,
    And tries the hydra-mob to tame ;
  While Patmore rocks a baby's cot
    And sings sweet nuptials void of blame.
  (Ah ! gentle Bards without a spot !
  Beshrew me if I envy not
    Such innocent and stainless fame !)
Next, though the rogues have wit in plenty,
  I still must pass politely by
The Savile bards, those four-and-twenty
  Blackbirds all piping in one pie !

I do not fancy Lewis Morris
  Would care for rhythmic freaks so strident—
Non sibi Venus mittit flores,
  Non sibi æquora ponti rident !
Matt Arnold seeks for 'light' no more
  But sleeps serene and satisfied ;
While Edwin, of that ilk, doth pore
On screeds of luminous Eastern lore
  By moonlight on the Ganges' side.
Dear Roden Noel, round whose throat
  Byron's loose collar still is worn,
Now tunes his song to one clear note
  Divinely gentle and forlorn ;
Far, far from him whom holy choirs
  Of angel infants stoop to kiss,
The stormy doubts, the fierce desires,
  Of questionable songs like this !
George Meredith might serve my turn
For thoughts that breathe and words that burn,
Or, better still, his master Browning,
  A sober'd Saul in evening dress ;
But both these bards would end by frowning
  At my mad Muse's gamesomeness.
No ! these respectable and gracious
  Bards with clean shirts will never do !
I need a spirit more audacious,
Morality more free and spacious,
  To inspire my song and help me through.

The world is tired of things poetic,
But poets are themselves to blame ;
Their wine's too sickly and emetic,
Or, grown too thin and dietetic,
It lacks the old flush of morning flame !
Far is the cry from Byron's brandy
To Pater's gods of sugar candy !
Lost the Homeric swing and trot,
Jingle of spur and beam of blade,
Of that moss-trooper, Walter Scott,
Riding upon his border raid,
And pricking south with all his power
To capture Shakespeare's feudal tower !
Where the swash-bucklers throng'd in force
The æsthete mounts his hobby horse,
And troubadours devoid of gristle
Play the French flute and Cockney whistle.
Sir Alfred only, gently glad,
Stainless and chaste as Galahad,
Clothed in white armour like a maid
Goes carolling through glen and glade,
Singing in silvern tones a song
Against the world of lust and wrong—
Certain, though all his fellows fail,
Of gaining the Parnassian Grail !

Peace with these poets one and all !
Flowers on their happy footsteps fall !

Yet would to Heaven their songs could be
More glad, more primitive and free!
Ah, for the days gone by! when Singers
Were wonder-workers, pleasure-bringers!
When Art was bold, when sunburnt Mirth
   Gladden'd around the Maypole leaping;
When the mad Muses tript the earth,
Not clad, as now, in silks by Worth,
   But gipsy-like and briskly skipping!
Then, skirts were lifted in the breeze
To show brown legs and lissome knees!
Then, men were hale and maids were merry,
   Then, Nature felt the breath of Spring;
Then, poets shouted 'Heydown Derry'
   And played at kisses-in-the-ring!
But when the trumpet-call rang round them
   Threw armour on and rode to fight,
Till in due time the people crown'd them—
   The Kings of Music, Mirth, and Might!

My Dedication?   Well, no more
I'll linger on this sunless shore,
Where prim landlubbers of the island
Go gathering shells of verse on dry land!
No! o'er the seas I sail, to seek
   My Homer of the southern seas,
Who, proudly pagan, Yankee-Greek,
   Flung out his banner to the breeze,

Then, wandering onward like Ulysses,
   Heard Syrens sing of Nature's charms
Leaping on shore to greet with kisses
The dainty dimpled nutbrown misses,
   Found the lost Eden in their arms !

To thee, O HERMANN MELVILLE, name
The surges trumpet into fame,
Last of the grand Homeric race,
   Great tale-teller of the marines,
I give this Song, wherein I chase
   Thy soul thro' magic tropic scenes !
Ah, would that I, poor modern singer,
Spell-bound with Care's mesmeric finger,
Might to the living world forth-figure
Thine Odyssean strength and vigour !
Alas ; o'er waves *you* tost on gladly
I sail more timidly and sadly,
And find no surcease or protection
From *mal de mer*, or introspection !   ·
Yet ne'er the less, in spite of all   ⌣
Mishaps and ills that may befall,
Despite the tumult and commotion,
   The countless shipwrecks of the time,
Away I go across the Ocean
   In this my cockleshell of rhyme !

Aid me, O sea-compelling man !

Before whose wand Leviathan
Rose white and hoary from the Deep,
With awful sounds that broke its sleep!
MELVILLE, whose magic brought Typee
Radiant as Venus from the Sea!
Who, ignorant of the draper's trade,
 Indifferent to the arts of dress,
Drew Fayaway the South-Sea maid
 Almost in mother-nakedness!
Without a robe, or boot, or stocking
(A want of clothes to some so shocking),
With just one chemisette to dress her,
She *lives*, and still shall live, God bless her!
Long as the Sea rolls deep and blue,
 While Heaven repeats the thunder of it,
Long as the White Whale ploughs it through,
The shape my Sea-Magician drew
 Shall still endure,—or I'm no prophet!

II.

OUT on the waters, lost in light,
His ship fades softly out of sight,
While on a beach of golden sands,
Shading his eyes with archèd hands
And gazing up to heights of palm,
Alone the dark-eyed Outcast stands
And breathes warm airs of spice and balm :
Behind him amethystine seas,
Just touch'd with shadows of the breeze,
Foam on the red-lip'd reefs that rise
Beyond the shallows rainbow-hued—
Before him, under burning skies,
Rise slopes of pine and sandalwood,
High as the topmost summit whère
A lonely palm-tree stirs its fan
Sharp-shadow'd 'gainst the golden glare
Of cloudless voids cerulean.
And downward from the wooded height
A torrent hangs its scarf of white,
A sparkling necklace that unfurls
Strung with for-ever-changing pearls,
Turning the sunlight in its fold
To rainbow beams and glints of gold.
And down beneath lie rounded huts
Tree-shaded, dusky, brown as nuts,

With lithe black figures moving slow
From sun to shadow to and fro:
And from the stillness all around
Comes now and then a distant sound
Of voices faint and far, that seem
As strange as voices heard in dream!

In the warm hush of summer weather,
    The tremulous hearts of Sky and Sea,
Like hearts of lovers prest together,
    Lie still, just throbbing peacefully—
And where they mix with sleepy sighs,
    Soft stirs of bliss and rapturous smile,
Upon the Sea's blue bosom lies
    This jewel of a coral Isle—
A dark green spot with gentle gleams
Of golden sands and silver streams,
With dusky depths of scented glade,
And cool wells bubbling in the shade;
And over all sleeps soft as balm
A glowing Paradisal calm.

Slowly, with shadow blotted black
    On the white sands, the Outcast moves,
Leaves the blue waters at his back
    And gains the quiet coca-groves.
His stormy heart scarce seems to beat,
    His troubled blood scarce seems to flow—

"The foliage trembling and astir
Is full of creatures warm and bright."—*Page* 81.

' If this were Death, then Death were sweet!'
　He murmurs in the golden glow.
Tall, dark, and strange, a stately form,
　He walks thro' woods of emerald green,
When suddenly the branches swarm
　With dusky faces mild of mien !
He pauses, starts, and looks around,—
The faces, vanish with no sound,
But 'mong the boughs he seems to hear
A sound like laughter merry and clear.
And presently, beside a pool
　Blue as a patch of fallen sky,
He stands, and in the mirror cool
　Sees shades of swift bright birds float by.
Upon the marge he sits, below
Acacia-branches white as snow,
And marks his own face worn with care
Uplooking from the waters there.
Suddenly, as he sits and broods,
　, Come laughter and soft chattering cries,
And mother-naked from the woods
　Steal dusky shapes with wondering eyes !
The tropic boughs, the flowery brakes,
Grow live with limbs that move like snakes,
Great open eyes 'mid opening flowers
Gleam out amid these shadowy bowers,
The foliage trembling and astir
　Is full of creatures warm and bright,

F

Who on the sad-eyed Mariner
   Gaze in mild wonder and delight !

He raised his melancholy eyes—
And back they shrank with bird-like cries—
But when he droop'd his head again
   And thro' the woods went wandering,
With speech as soft as summer rain,
   Voices that seem'd to sigh or sing,
They murmur'd to him in a tongue
   Most sweet yet scarce articulate,
Such as was heard when Love was young
   And Adam coo'd to woo his mate !
All vows, all vowels, language such
   As bees might use if they could tell
Their tremulous thrills of taste and touch
   Deep in some honeysuckle's cell ;
Murmur of insects and of birds,
Just turning joy to honied words,—
Half human speech, half speechless cadence,
   Voluptuous as the time and place,
And rapturous as some rosy maiden's
   Sigh, when she yields to Love's embrace.

The simile in that last line
Is Vanderdecken's (and not mine)
Ta'en, from the Notebook written in
His own red blood on parchment skin.

Henceforward, that the reader may
  Avoid confounding his reflections
With mine, I'll use throughout my lay
  His own remarks and interjections.
So understand, whene'er I quote
  Passages some consider shocking,
Inverted commas will denote
  'Tis only Vanderdecken mocking!

" I turn'd—they vanish'd, with a sound
  Like music of some scented shower
That ceases on warm grassy ground,
While all the green boughs rustle round
  And bright drops cling on leaf and flower.
But as I wander'd from the shade
  The happy creatures follow'd after,
Clear voices ran in the green glade
  Answer'd with rippling peals of laughter!
And when into the sun I strode
  They ring'd me round with throngs at gaze,
As if they looked upon a god
  In mingled worship and amaze!

" Then one, with laughter low yet clear,
  Ran from the rest to interview me,
But paused at arm's length full of fear
  And turn'd a wistful face unto me—-
Beauteous, à woman yet a child,

Her gentle eyes upon me bent
With humid orbs both sweet and mild,
She stretch'd a little hand, then smiled
　In welcome and in wonderment !
And lo, as if a fountain's dew
　Was scatter'd on my brows and hair,
Refresh'd and gladdening ere I knew,
I felt the smile, and, smiling too,
　Shook off the cloud of my despair !

" Venus ! *Natura procreans !*
　Te, Dea, adventumque tuum,
All living things obey, and Man's
Proud spirit vainly plots and plans
　Thy spells to scatter, and break through 'em !
A look—a smile—a touch—suffices
　To witch our nature and to win it—
Stone turns to merry flesh, and ice is
　Wine warm and rosy in a minute !
So was it then, so is it ever,
Spite all Morality's endeavour !
So shall it be, though parsons patter,
As long as Man is two-thirds Matter !
Won by the face and form of her
　Who welcomed me for all the rest,
I felt my stony heart astir
　And throbbing gently in my breast.
I took her little hand,—and gazed

Into her eyes with kindly greeting;
Hers did not drop, but, softly raised,
  Sparkled with pleasure at the meeting!
And full of joy, no longer flying
  The strange sad form from distant lands,
Her dusty kinsfolk, laughing, crying,
  Flock'd round about with outstretch'd hands;
Women and men and children small,
  Dusky and gentle, old and young,
Welcomed the stranger,—one and all
Uttering the same soft bird-like call,
  And prattling in that golden tongue;
And what I fail'd to understand
  The kindly folk made bright and clear
By smile of face and touch of hand,
  Which said, ' O Stranger, welcome here ! '
For they had never seen before
A white man on that sunny shore,
And to their gaze I seem'd to be
Clothed round with grace of Deity!
A little bored, a little scorning,
  I gazed with calm superior air
On these wild Children of the Morning
  Happy with scarce a rag to wear;
And some were comely, all were bright
With life and innocent delight,
And never one among the throng
Suspected cruelty or wrong:

Happy as beasts or birds, unstricken
   With modern psychical disease,
Free of complaints whereof souls sicken,
They felt the sun within them quicken
   And lived the life of swarming bees :
Their very speech, as I have said,
   Scarce consonanted, clear and sweet
As warm winds whispering overhead,
   As runlets rippling at their feet,—
Beauteously fitted to express
Anacreontic happiness,
One cooing and delicious tone,
Like that to Grecian lovers known,
Ὀμφήν λιγεῖαν προχέων.

" And so, as on a flowery stream
One floateth in a summer dream,
Upon this flow of lives, swept round
   By merry maids and children gay,
'Mid soft delights of scent and sound,
   I floated and was borne away—
From shade to sun, from sun to shade,
   Laughing they led me thro' the land,
And still that dimpled dainty Maid
Nestled quite close, and unafraid
   Smiled in my face and kiss'd my hand.
And laughing too, while on me fell
The golden glamour and the spell,

I wander'd on at their sweet will !—
  O had I power to paint the scene,
Not scribbling with this blood-stain'd quill,
  But with a brush of sweep serene !—
I, the sad Man with dark locks shed
  Round features worn and marble pale,
My lithe form strangely garmented
  In raiment wrought to brave the gale ;
Rings on my waxen hands ; around
My throat a bright scarf lightly wound ;
On broad brows beaten by the sea
A sailor's hat worn jauntily !
The centre of the picture, this ;
  Around, dark Darlings of the Isle,
Warm bosoms panting full of bliss,
Waists to embrace and lips to kiss,
  And best, that Maiden's sunny smile !
Thus was I tangled in the mesh
  Of those bright moving living bowers !
The sun shone free, the wind blew fresh,
  And Eden smiled, all fruit, all flowers !
Far off, beyond the emerald land
Sloping to shores of yellow sand,
Beyond the stately coca trees
Stirring their fans in the soft breeze,
Past the red coral reef whereon
  The turquoise Sea broke milky white,
Far as my dazzled eyes could con

Ocean and Heaven mingling shone,—
Veil beyond veil of golden light !

" And now we come to swarms of huts
Dusky and brown as coca-nuts,
Beneath a crag that skyward towers
Festoon'd from crown to base with flowers :
Some high, like great brown birds'-nests, clinging
High up and with the tree-boughs swinging,
Some fallen like husks of fruit and lying
    Wide open on the grassy sward ;
And hither and thither, multiplying
Like happy bees in sunlight flying,
    Fresh flocks of happy creatures pour'd,
Until the place was all alive
With forms that swarm'd from hive to hive,
Buzzing and murmuring every one
In that soft lingo of the Sun !

" Close to the flowery crag there clung
A brown thatch'd roof with wild flowers hung,
Supported on four sapling trees
That pour'd sweet scents on the warm breeze,
And underneath it, loosely wall'd
With boughs as green as emerald,
There lay a wide and open bower,
A mossy nest of fruit and flower,
With soft green hammocks swinging high

To the wind's summer lullaby.
Grass was the floor, but o'er it spread,
Crumbling warm spice beneath the tread,
Were woven carpets green and soft
As the fresh blooms that swung aloft.
Thither my captor, that sweet Maid
　Who held me in her sweet control.
Led me, and, seated in the shade,
　My throne an old tree's mossy bole,
I watch'd the throng who round me went
In welcome and in merriment.

" Possession's nine points of the law,
　Even yonder in the southern seas !
And murmuring softly ' Aloha !'
　(Which means ' I love you,' if you please !)
That Maid who was the first to capture
　My idle eyes with her strange beauty
Gazed on my face in tender rapture
　And kiss'd my hand in sign of duty.
Then, when some others, gladsome girls
With sunny cheeks and teeth like pearls,
Came thronging all around to view
My face and give me welcome too,
She waved them back with flashing eyes
　And seem'd to say (if looks could do it)
' This man is mine ! I claim the prize,
　And if you touch him, you shall rue it !'

Smiling and laughing merrily,
I just look'd on, content to be
Appropriated for the present
By one so young and plump and pleasant;
And nodding, by my side I placed her,
Patted her brown back and embraced her,—
Whereon the happy native bands,
  Incapable of jealous spite,
Laugh'd their approval, clapt their hands,
  And shared the little Maid's delight.

" Then, at a signal from the Maid,
  They brought me *poi*, a native dish
Of island grains and juices made,
  And stickier than one might wish—
Her two forefingers lightly dipping
  Therein, she twirled them round about,
Then drew a glutinous, slimy, dripping
  Mouthful, like macaroni, out ;
Next, quickly raised her finger-tips
Thus coated to her rosy lips,
Sucking them like a bonbon, while
I watch'd her with a wondering smile.
Ev'n thus she show'd me full of joy
The native mysteries of *poi*—
And presently, I made essay
To eat it in the native way,
And found the flavour of the stuff

(Altho' the *modus operandi*
Was strange and primitive enough),
    Was much like rice and sugar-candy.
And next they brought in goblets green
    Of coca-shell a pleasant tipple
As clear as mead or Hippocrène
    Or milk that flows from Venus' nipple;
And quaffing this right joyously
    I felt my heart within throb quicker,
For, like most sailors of the sea,
    I on occasion love good liquor!
And thus they fêted me and fed me,
    And when at last I paused contented,
To a green couch the Maiden led me,
    And down I sank on leaves sweet-scented;—
When nimble virgins, at her sign,
    Kneaded me, limbs and loins and thighs,
Till rack'd and rent I sank supine
    With aching frame and sleepy eyes,—
And sank to charmèd sleep! (They name
This swift shampooing of the frame
The *lomi-lomi.*) When at last
    I woke, all sense seem'd sublimated,
Bathed in a comfort deep and vast
    I lay like Adam new-created—
Ambrosial peace and perfect rest
    Stole through my veins and warm'd me through,
Serenely strong, completely blest,

I gladden'd at each breath I drew ;
And all the world and its annoy
Turn'd to an odorous rose of joy,
Taking both soul and sense in capture
With soft celestial folds of rapture !

" Meantime her kinsfolk, blithe and gay
As motes that in the sunbeam play,
Simple as babies biting coral,
Without one instinct known as moral,
Eager to welcome and caress
   Whatever stranger they beheld,
Full of the sunny happiness
   That from their dusky hearts up-well'd,
Came smiling round the flowery nest
Wherein I lay in blissful rest.
Then one, an Elder of the place,
A glad old boy with wrinkled face,
Laugh'd and clapt hands, and at the sign
All squatted down or lay supine,
And from the shade of these dark bowers
   Outpour'd, with wondrous twists and twirls,
Most lightly raimented in flowers
   A band of lissome Dancing Girls—
These, [while the rest began to croon
A drowsy droning native tune,]
With gestures loose and looser raiment,
With postures never for broad day meant,

With panting mouths and shining eyes,
With heaving breasts and quivering thighs,
Began a measure which to see
Would shock our modern modesty !
A measure ?—nay, a dance that knew
No measure Thought could time it to—
A leaping, eddying, unabating
Revel of flesh and blood pulsating—
Now soft and sweet as fountains falling,
    Now mad and wild as billows bounding,
Now murmurous as wood-doves calling,
Now corybantic and appalling,
    And changeful as it was astounding ! "

Reflections on the margin, made
    In Rome, at a quite recent time,
Follow, and tho' I'm half afraid
    To quote them, here they are, in rhyme :

. . . " Aye me, what witchery may be wrought
    By soft round arms and looks of passion !
What magic flooding sense and thought
    By limbs in beauteous undulation !
Love rules the world, and Love shall rule it,
Tho' rogues corrupt and sages fool it !
Love moves the chessmen, Kings and Knights,
    And stirs the merest pawns as well,
Hence change of empires, bloodiest fights,

And all the game of Heaven and Hell.
Herodias dances, and demands
   The Baptist's head as instant payment!
Phryne just stirs her little hands,
   Lifting the edge of her light raiment,
Glimpse of trim ankles to discover,
And lo! a Dynasty is over!
Were I the Devil, I'd rather deal
   With incantation such as this is,
Than have great senates at my heel!
Show me whole legions clad in steel—
   I'll rout them easily—with kisses!
Kings for such guerdon will pay down
Gladly the sceptre and the crown!
Bishops their mitres and their crosiers
For soft limbs beautified by hosiers!
God gets no hearing anywhere
While Womankind is fond and fair,
And so the world is at the mercy
Of the supreme enchantress, Circe!

   " Hartmann, whose page explains to us
The creed of the Unconscious,
By the Unconscious means the Power
Which fills Life's Tree from root to flower.
Pulsating out of yonder sunlight,
   Flowing in flame from form to form,
Is the eternal Light, the one Light

For ever wanton, wild, and warm,—
Shedding magnetic rays of splendour,
In ecstasies of new creation,
Forcing all creatures to surrender
To Love's amphibious invitation!
Amœbæ in the ooze, and fishes,
Beasts in the fields, birds in the air,
Sweep whither the Unconscious wishes,
And recreate forms foul or fair—
All sing *Natura Cumulans,*—
Nature, the Matronhood immortal—
In vain *le bon Dieu* sits and plans
Yonder beyond the heavenly portal,
Crying like Canute, to the Ocean
Of loose primordial mad emotion,
' Thus far, no further '—while its waves,
Beating the shore of human graves,
Surging and rising, ever growing,
Submerging earth from zone to zone,
Drown Man's frail Soul, and overflowing
Flood the bright Footstool of the Throne ! "

Wide-eyed in wonder and delight
The Wanderer drank in the sight—
A Bacchic rite in emulation
Of the first orgies of Creation !
And when the dancers sunk o'erpower'd
With their own rapture, blossoms shower'd

Upon them, and with flashing faces . .
They clung in beautiful embraces.
Then when the cup of joy was full
    Up to the brim and running over,
Out of the darkness green and cool
    A girl coo'd clearly to her lover :—
One bird-like note, one plaintive call,
Passionate yet celestial,
Thrill'd through the silence ! then there came
    Out of the darkness, robed in white,
With arms outstretch'd and eyes aflame,
    Alive with Love and Love's delight,
That Flower of Maidens,—fair she stood
Full in the sunset's crimson flood,
And gazing on the heavens above
Warbled her wondrous song of Love !
And fascinated, thrilling through
With bliss at every breath he drew,
The Outcast listen'd, while the throng
Were hushed to hear that Orphic song !
'But as he leapt to her embrace
    She laugh'd and vanish'd from his glance,
And once again the leafy place
    Was loud with life and song and dance—
Again, while loud the music rung,
The choir of dancing girls upsprung,
And mingling in the measure wrought
Their fine gyrations passion-fraught !

But now the dance was less capricious,
  The undulations more subdued,—
Subsiding into throbs delicious,
  Faint rapture stealing through their blood,
The maidens moved like one bright billow
  Now heavenward, now upon the ground,
All swaying on an airy pillow
  And swooning with soft zones unbound,
And spicy odours, burning beams,
Blew round them as they rock'd in dreams,
While on their happy cheeks and eyes
Rain'd diamond dews from Paradise !

A pause—a thrill—which seem'd to be
A long sweet dream of ecstasy—
Then suddenly, before he knew,
All vanish'd from his wondering view—
Of all the throng not one was there,
Men, women, maidens, turn'd to air,
And lonely on his couch he lay
Lit by the sunset's fading ray—
But as he sigh'd and lookt around,
  He heard again that bird-like cadence
And turning saw, with lilies crown'd,
  That tender miracle of maidens—
Her eyes on his—one soft hand prest
To still the billowing of her breast—
Her cheeks all smiles, her eyes all bliss,

G

Sending new thrills of rapture through him,
Her mouth bent down for him to kiss,
Her soul a votive offering to him!

Then Twilight spread its purple fold
    Dew-spangled o'er the blue sky's bosom,
And ripe and large as fruit of gold
    Great sun-fed stars began to blossom,—
Such stars as never kindle save
Out yonder o'er the tropic wave,
    Each like a little moon, and making
    In the smooth Ocean trails of light,
While others, from the darkness breaking
Like bursting fruit, shot seaward shaking
    Prismatic splendours through the night.
As each new splendour flashed afar
    And melted in the quiet Main,
It seem'd as if some shining star
    Had burst within the Wanderer's brain!
And spicy scents of that green Land
    On the warm wind were wafted thither,
As holding that dark Maiden's hand,
    Silent he sat, uplooking with her.
Then sighing heavily, he turn'd
His dark eyes shoreward, and discern'd
The spume upon the reef that fell
Like white milk from the coca-shell,
The waters round of lustre green

Alive with rays of starry sheen,
And far off, on the water's bound,
The Moon uprising large and round,
Clear lemon-yellow, without rays,
Out of the pathless ocean-ways !

III.

HE turned his eyes on that sweet Maid,
Who smiling in his face essay'd
Quick eager speech of rippling words
    More musical than any singer's,—
He guess'd the meaning of the words
    By the warm pressure of the fingers !
Child-like she stood, with eyes of light
Full of the happy tropic night,
A white straw hat upon her head
With ferns and flowers bright-garlanded,
Her dress one cool chemise of snow
    Wherein her soft form slipt at ease,
Sleeveless, around the breasts cut low,
    And fluttering to the supple knees ;
Her limbs and arms all bare and warm,
    Her bosom gently palpitating,—
Her face alive with Love, her form
    Thrill'd through with fires of Love's creating !

Over that night now falls the veil !
Earth held her breath.   The stars grew pale
Down-gazing.   Heavenly balms were strewn
On those two forms who 'neath the Moon
Took Love's divine first kiss.   The Night
Linger'd above them in delight,

Till softly and serenely blest,
Still as two love-birds in a nest,
They slept ! . . .
        O Alohà ! (which means
' I love you,' mind) delightful Maiden !
Still in the daintiest of your teens,
   Yet woman-soul'd and passion-laden !
Through you, alas ! I make this canto
More warmly-colour'd than I want to !
For I profess—let all men know it—
To be a Psychologic Poet !
Not that with solemn cogitations
I mean to tire the reader's patience,
Hair-splitting and refining ether
Like *some* bards (and no small ones neither)
Who show with philosophic hiccup
The metaphysics in a teacup,
And plummets deep as Death apply
To gauge the depths of apple-pie !
But aiming at the adumbration
Of Nature's chaos of sensation,
The more I of these Mysteries speak
The more I pause with blushing cheek !
Many will misconceive me ; some
Will just be thunderstruck and dumb
That I should dream of spiritualising
A subject which—there's no disguising—
Is delicate extremely.   Then

I dread the Critics, those small men
With those big voices! . . .
                              Furthermore,
The days of passionate song are o'er,
And now no Poet wins the laurel
Who is not absolutely moral.
We've had our fill of impropriety,
Since Byron rose to shock Society,
And of all moods by bards affected
Anacreon's has been least neglected.
The favourite Muses, Greek or British,
Have ever been extremely skittish,
And modern bards have drunk too wildly
The warm Greek wine which Goethe mildly
Sipt at while sketching with soft shade his
Loose-laced, lax-moral'd German ladies ;
Gretchen, Philina, all the crew,
Fleshly yet sentimental too,
Sad sensuous things of scant decorum,
Lost like the Magdalen before 'em,
Save Mignon, who, as story teaches,
Lack'd fat and so became the breeches.
Then we've had Byron, that lame Cupid
Of odalisques sublimely stupid,
Not to name here Chateaubriand,
Alfred de Musset, and George Sand,
All watering with artistic squirt
The flower of passion grown in dirt,

Till Gautier made the Immortals flutter
By rolling Venus in the gutter!
But patience! this strange tale I tell,
Is high as Heaven, though deep as Hell,
And in the end shall please the mind
That's to analysis inclined;
Shall show you, ere the last sad line,
The great Eternal Feminine
(Das Ewigweibliche, to wit,
As amorous Wolfgang christen'd it),
And vindicate its flights immodest
Through scenes where Venus lies unbodiced,
By flying on with fearless pinions
To the clear air of God's dominions.

That night, within their bower of bloom
Flooded with moonlight and perfume,
The Captain and his new-found treasure
Drank deep of Love's o'erflowing measure,
Then down the Unconscious sinking deep
Floated on shimmering seas of Sleep.

Wonder and hush miraculous!
    When, weary of her load of care,
This Earth, whose fond arms shelter us,
    Feels softly on her brows and hair
The cool dark dews of twilight fall
Mysterious and celestial!

Lo! while her golden robe of day
Slips film by film and falls away,
Naked and warm she stands a space,
The sun-flush fading from her face:
Then, with bow'd head and soft hands prest
Upon her bare and billowing breast,
Takes, while the chill Moon steals in sight,
The cold ablution of the Night!
And then, as by the pools of rest
She lieth down subdued and blest,
As on her closèd eyes are shed
Dim influence from the heavens o'erhead,
We nestling in her bosom close
Our feverish eyelids and repose—
Our spirits husht, our voices dumb,
    Our little lives a little still'd,
We sleep!—and round us softly come
    Souls from whose fountains ours are fill'd!
Spirits as soft as moonbeams flit
Around our rest, not breaking it,
Brushing across our lips and eyes
Wings wet with dews of Paradise!
While at God's mercy and at theirs
We lie, they bless us unawares,—
Watch the Soul's pool that lies within
The branches dark of Flesh and Sin,
And stir it as with Aaron's rod
To gleams of Heaven and dreams of God!

Lifting the filmy tent of Sleep
With gentle fingers, on us peep
Those errant angels, soft and tender
With some strange starlight's dusky splendour ;
With balm from Heaven they bedew us,
Bring flowers from Heaven and hold them to us,
Flash on our eyes the diamonds shaken
To fairy rainbows as we waken,
And jubilantly ere departing
  Ring those wild echoes in our ears,
Which, flusht and from our pillows starting,
  We hearken for with childish tears !

If Dreams were *not,* if we could fall
To slumber and not dream at all,—
If when the eyes were closed, the sense
Close shut, all seeing vanish'd thence,
Why, 'twere not difficult to fancy
This life no freak of necromancy,—
And Man a clock, contrived to go
(Bar breakage) seventy years or so,
Yet running down and pausing nightly,
  Pendulum fluttering with no pain,
Till, as the daydawn glimmers brightly,
  A Finger quickens it again !
But Dreams, though sages think them silly,
Attest us Spirits willy-nilly,
And prove that, when the Unconscious glides

Around us with its numbing tides,
Shapes past conceiving or control
Stir the dark cisterns of the Soul!
All day God veils Himself in Light,
But down the starry stairs each night
He steals with solemn soundless tread
And finds us—fast asleep, not dead!
Ah, then begins the conjuration,
The Mystery, the Incantation!
The Feet Divine with soft insistence
Plash through the Waters of Existence,
Send strange electric thrills each minute
Down to the very ooze within it,
While, startled by the shining Presence,
All Nature breaks to phosphorescence! . . .

Now came the golden tropic Morning!
 Not like our dawns of chilly gloom:
One glow, one crimson flash of warning,
 Then one great flood of blinding bloom—
The world awoke and leapt—the Sea
Flasht like a mirror radiantly—
The leaves and flowers were all alive—
 A miracle of Light was done—
And glad as bees from out the hive
 The people flock'd into the sun!

Happy, contented, and serene,

ALOHA.—*Page 106.*

The Outcast left his nuptial bed,
While, blushing like a happy queen,
His bride just kissed his lips and fled,—
But soon tript back on lightsome feet:
With troops of maidens in her train,
Bringing her lord fresh fruits to eat
And cups of coca-milk to drain.
Then gay and glad he sought the strand
And stript, and plung'd into the tide,
And, striking strongly out from land
In pools of Dawn beatified,
He heard a rippling laugh, and turning
Saw her behind him, swimming too—
Her dusky face upon him yearning
Baptized with joy and morning dew!

That was the Dawn, the bright beginning
Of one long day of Love's delight!
Happy, unconscious she was sinning,
His slave by day, his bride by night,
She, with her people's acquiescence,
Said in Love's language, 'I am thine,'
And happy in her constant presence
He lived and loved and felt divine!
And ah! what wonder he was glad,
That all his soul grew iridescent,
Forgot the past so dark and sad,
With such a Bride for ever present?

Soft almond eyes of starry splendour,
   Lips poppy-red, teeth white as pearls,
A warm brown cheek sun-tan'd and tender,—
   The nicest, nakedest of girls!
Her form from shoulder down to foot
   Like Cupid's bow a splendid curve,
Her flesh as soft as ripen'd fruit
   Yet quick with quivering pulse and nerve—
Her limbs, like those of some fair statue,
   Perfectly rounded, strong yet slight,
Her childish glance, when smiling at you,
   Alive with luxury of light!
O happy he whose head could rest
Upon that warm and bounteous breast,
And so ecstatically capture
Its tropic indolence of rapture!
How darkly, passionately fair
She seem'd when, resting by him there
Upon a couch of leaves sweet-scented,
   She smiled without a single care,
And took no kiss that she repented,
   And knew no thought he could not share.
And when he wearied with the light
Shed on his dazzled soul and sight,
Still as a bird within the nest
She saw his dark eyes close in rest;
And lay beside him fondly waiting,
   Obedient as a happy child,

Watching his face, and palpitating
  Till he awoke again and smiled !
For all her pleasure was to trace
The happiness upon his face,
To feel his breath flow warmly thro' her,
To kiss his hands and draw them to her,
And place them on her heart, that he
Might feel it leaping happily !
And ever springing from his side,
  She brought him fruit and dainties sweet,
And knelt beside him, happy-eyed
  To see her Lord and Master eat—
And if he frown'd her face grew very
Sad ; if he laugh'd, her face grew merry ;
So every shade of his emotion
  Past to her face and faithful eyes,
As shadows of the summer Ocean
  Answer the changes of the Skies !

A Rose with Dawn's cool dew and savour
Renew'd at every kiss he gave her,
A Blush Rose passionately scented,
Serene, unconscious, and contented,
She felt soft airs of Heaven bedew her,
And drank their sweetness deep into her,
Kept Soul and Body, through light and glooming,
One Flower for ever freshly blooming !

O happy Life !   O blissful Passion !

Far from Life's folly and Life's fashion !

Far from the tailor and the hatter !

 Far from the clubs and criticasters !

Far from all metaphysic patter,

From all cold creeds of God and Matter,

 From silly sheep and sillier pastors !

No Parliaments,. to lying given—

 No paupers, and no governing classes—

No books, or newspapers, thank Heaven !

 And no God Jingo for the masses !

O happy Life, without a trouble !

Pure and prismatic as a bubble,

 Fresh as a flower with dewdrops pearl'd,—

Ere naked *Truth* rose, with a wink,

Black from her Well (of printer's ink)

 Or out of chaos woke the *World !*

IV.

Pause, Moral Reader, ere you scold
A Bard that seemeth overbold,
And grasp the truth that I who sing
Am like my Hero wandering
Outlaw'd and lost ! Let me commend you,
Moreover, should the theme offend you,
To realize that he whose tale
  I tell was ' damn'd ' (right justly too),—
Forgetting this, you'll wholly fail
  To gain the proper point of view.

For your assistance, I'll again
  Quote from the Note-book, thus translating :

" How peaceful, after all the pain
  Of endless doubting and debating !
How restful, after stormy grief,
This quiet of the lotus-leaf !
And yet, and yet ! how Memory flashes
  Her mirror in my sleepy eyes,
While darkly on my drooping lashes
  The tear-drops linger as they rise !
I mark the Land where I was born,
  The red-tiled Town beside the sea,—
The Mother who awakes at morn

And turns to give her kiss—to *me !*
I walk along the sun-brown'd sands,
I gather sea-shells in my hands,
I run and sport till death of day,
Then kneeling by my cot, I pray. . . .
Again I am a fisher-lad,
   I haul the net, I trim the sail,
I whistle to the winds, right glad
    To hear the gathering of the gale.
Then sailing homeward tan'd and brown
I watch the red lights of the Town
Gleam blur'd and moist thro' mist and rain,
While down the anchor merrily goes again !
I leap on land, run up the shore,
Eager to gain my home once more,
And startle with a boy's delight
   The widow'd Mother waiting there !
Almighty God ! that night, that night !
   Ev'n now it chokes me with despair !
For lo, I see the thin white form
   Stretch'd on the bed in ghastly rest,
The lips clay cold that once were warm,
   The frail hands folded on the breast—
Mother ! my mother ! even now,
I bend and kiss thy marble brow,
The boy's heart breaks, the salt tears flow,
And the great Storm of human Woe
Sweeps round the quick and dead !—Aye me,

That first great grief, the worst of all !
That first despair and agony,
To which all later woes seem small !

" Then first I knew Thee, God ! whose breath
Is felt in pestilence of Death !
Then first I knew Thee whom men bless
And found Thee blind and pitiless !
I knew and lived—for 'twas Thy will
Only to torture, not to kill—
And so the torn heart heal'd at last,
And I survived, but not the same—
And ere the sense of sorrow pass'd
The life within me broke to flame
Of Youth's first love !—and I forgot
The woe which is our mortal lot,
Because a maiden's face was fair,
Because a maiden's lips were sweet,—
She bound me with her golden hair
And threw me captive at her feet.
Then, the glad wooing ! The new birth
Of man and God, of Heaven and Earth,
When softly, thro' the shades of night
We stole and watch'd the evening star,
While faint and distant, flashing white,
Waves murmur'd from the harbour bar.
How good Thou wast, Almighty One,
Blessing my troth, the maiden's vow !

H

But ere another year was done
 I curst Thee, as I curse Thee now.
For lo, Thine Angel Death past by,
 With flaming finger touched her breast—
Scarce woman yet, too young to die,
 She sicken'd of a vague unrest,
Till on her lips clung day by day
The blood-phlegm ever wiped away
By the thin kerchief, while she tried
 To force the smile that fought with tears—
God, hear my curse once more!—She *died,*—
 But still, across the raging years,
Her wan face rises, to proclaim
Her Maker's infamy and shame!

"Pass all the rest!—My Soul knew then
The hourly martyrdom of men,
And turn'd in very impotence
To books for comfort, gathering thence
(For they had taught me how to read)
The lies and lusts of every creed.
Then, an old Scribe, who loved to pore
On pages of forbidden lore,
Gave me, for service gently done,
 The knowledge that I long'd to gain,
Good soul!—he used me like his son,
 And made me erudite and vain.
Four years of this, in Rotterdam,

Combin'd with studies less improving,
And I became the thing I am,
Worn with much thinking and much loving,
For in that City women were
As bountiful as they were fair.
Then, suffering from an accidental
Complaint to lovers detrimental,
I passed some time, just for variety,
  'Mong doctors in the Hospital—
Then, tired of land and she-society,
  Cried ' Curse the women ! one and all ! '
And off again I went, as sailor
Before the mast, upon a Whaler.
' Gentleman Phil ' they had me christen'd,
  For I could curse in French and Greek,
And merrily the rascals listen'd
  When I discoursed, with tongue in cheek,
On men and women, God and Matter,
  And all things wicked and unclean !
Lord, how they loved my learnéd patter,
  My blasphemies and jokes obscene !

" Long after, came my Luck. Despairing
Of gaining much by pure sea-faring,
I join'd some honest men and brothers
  Who robbed upon the Wet Highway,
And being cleverer than the others
  I gathered gold, as rascals may—

Grown rich, I earn'd their approbation
  By deeds acurst they dared not do,
And being skill'd in navigation,
And of some little education,
  Became the Captain of the crew.
By Heaven and Hell, those days were merry!
  We knew no pity, felt no fear,—
Devils that played at hey down derry
  With all that honest men hold dear!
Nor were the smiles of Venus wanting,
  For many a fat ship was our prize,
And many a woman most enchanting
Struck her red blush-flag, and sank panting
  Under our fire of amorous eyes. . . .
Ah deeds acurst! Do I repent?
  Perhaps a little, now and then!
But what was *God* about, who sent
Things that were pure and innocent
  To be the spoil of beast-like men?"

Much in this not too pious vein
The crimson leaves o' the Book contain—
Much, too, of scenes which would have staggered
Jules Verne or Mr Rider Haggard,
So full they were of wind and water,
Clangour of swords, and general slaughter.
But presently we find him pining
  To slip his fetters and be free,

On beds of amaranth reclining
  With eyes upon the turquoise sea.

"So, as I've said, or just suggested,
  I, the crass Outcast of the Lord,
Seeking salvation (as requested),
In that first Haven snugly nested,
  Was rapidly becoming bored.
The Honeymoon, I've always thought,
  Is a mistake! I'd tire, I swear,
If in the net of Wedlock caught,
  Of Venus' self, the ever Fair!
No, 'tis the wooing and the winning,
Not the long end, but the beginning,
That is the joy of Love!—Mere courting
Passes all amorous disporting,
And what we crave contains a blessing
We never compass in possessing!
Some men, I grant (not damn'd like me)
Are arm'd so strong in purity,
That wedlock is an endless boon,
And life one long-drawn Honeymoon,—
And these appease their modest wishes
As peacefully as jelly-fishes,
And floating flaccid 'neath the sky
Tamely increase and multiply.
But these are fish-like things, not Lovers,
Spawn of the pools, not Ocean-rovers,

Lives drifting where the currents choose,
Or sunk in matrimonial ooze.
Moreover, I who write had sown
My wild oats early, and had known
All kinds of pleasure, long before
My rotten Barque set out from shore.
And when the Master of Creation,
Or some blind Force, his adumbration,
Gave me the chance to find salvation
Somewhere on earth,—I steer'd despairing
  To this soft Eden in the seas,
And nothing hoping, nothing caring,
  Thought 'Here at least I'll rest at ease !'
Not to the Cities did I wander,
Not to the Schools where pedants ponder,
Not to the tents of Civilization,
But back, straight back, to nude Creation !—
And here I found the general Mother
  Beauteous and bounteous, warm and wild,
And from her heart, like many another,
  I drank Life's milk, a happy child.
My blessing on her !   Grand and free,
Untainted with morality,
With but one Law of life and pleasure
  To render her supremely blest,
She gives me all she hath, full measure
  Of that great Milky Way, her Breast—
Yet though I linger here, replete

As any flower with all that's sweet,
I often long to be once more
A foam-fleck blown from shore to shore!"

A " London " Note—" How faint to-day
Seems all, that Eden far away!
Ev'n then that life, such as the pure hope
  To find at last beyond the sky,
Was far removed from life in Europe
  And all the scandal and the cry
Of life in Cities!—People there
  Were naked babies sucking corals,
Spent blissful days without a care,
Had no idea what morals were,
  And so—were innocent of morals.
Since then the Gospel has been spread there,
And divers bad complaints been shed there,
And Civilization's boisterous busy hum
Has quite destroyed that sweet Elysium.
Soon, if the natives keep progressing,
  They'll turn to Scandal for variety,
Receive the new god Jingo's blessing,
Become æsthetic in their dressing,
  And have their Journals of Society!"

Another, blasphemous and fierce.
" Oft, when I think of that fair place,
  I front the heavens and seek to pierce,

O God, Thy cloudy hiding-place.
For mark, ev'n there, unseen by me,
  Thy Deputies, Disease and Death,
Were crawling snake-like from the sea
  To taint pure Nature with their breath.
There, tangled in Thy mesh of woes,
Tortured and stain'd the Leper rose,
And join'd his wail to all the cries
That from the host of martyrs rise
High as Thy Throne !   Tell me, Thou God,
Who, striking Chaos with Thy rod,
Creating Heaven, and Earth, and Flood,
Praised Thine own work and call'd it ' good,'
Tell me, O God, if God Thou art,
Doth Thy Hand rend the breaking heart
In beasts and men, doth it adjust
The Hate of Hate, the Lust of Lust,
And blotch Thy work, Humanity,
With these foul stains of Leprosy !
What art Thou, God, if this be so ?
  What is the glory Thou dost claim ?—
Thy tribute is eternal woe,
  Thy pride eternal Death and shame !
I toss the gauge to Thee again !
  Unfold Thyself, defend Thy plan,—
Or own Thy primal work was vain,
And let Thy tears descend like rain
  To attest Thy sin at making Man ! "

" We feel too much, we know too little,
    We gaze behind us and before ;
The magic wand of Faith, grown brittle,
    Breaks in our grasp ; our Dream is o'er !
Wakening at last, we understand
The World's no pretty Fairyland,
No sunny World with gods above it,
No happy World with God to love it,
But a worn World whose first sweet prayer
Is turned to darkness and despair—
A World without a God !—

            " O Mother,
    We cling to thee with feeble cries,
Fight for thy breast with one another,
    Or wondering watch thy sightless eyes
Upturn'd to Heaven !—O Mother Earth,
Still fair and kind as at thy birth,
Still tender yet forlorn, as when
Out of thy womb the race of men
Came crying—with the same sad cry
That haunts thee while they droop and die !
Sad as the Sphynx, and blind ! for *thou*
    Hast look'd *once* on the Father's face,
Hast felt His kiss upon thy brow,
    Hast quicken'd, too, in His embrace,
Till blind with light of Deity

That clasp'd thee and was mix'd with thee,
Thine eyes for ever ceasod to see ;
And night by night and day by day
Patiently thou dost grope thy way,
Clasping thy children, heavenward,
    In search of Him who comes no more—
O Mother ! patient ! evil-star'd !
Who now shall be Thy stay and guard,
    Now that first Dream of Love is o'er ?

" Thy children babble of green fields !
    Thy youth and maidens, gladly crying,
Suck all the sweets that Nature yields,
    And lie i' the sun, as I am lying !
They learn the raptures of the sense,
Break Love's ripe virgin gourd and thence
Drink the fresh waters of delight . . .
What then ?   To-morrow Death and Night
Shall find them, or if Death denies
The boon which closes weary eyes,
Despair more dire than Death shall come
To linger o'er their martyrdom !
O Mother ! martyred too !—yet blest
To feel the new-born at thy breast,
What of thy Dead ?   What of the prayers
Taught them of old to still their cares ?

What of the promise fondly given
Of comfort, and a Father in Heaven ?
There is no God ! there is no Father !
And that which clasp'd thee, mother Earth,
Was formless, voiceless, monstrous, rather
Than gracious and of heavenly birth—
The attributes we take from *thee*
Are bright and fair, tho' only clay,—
The living force that keeps us free,
The joy of Life, the bliss of Day !
What we inherit from the Sire
Is formless, passionless, and dim,
Deep dread, despair, unrest, desire
To climb the heavens and gaze on Him !
Ah, hopeless and eternal quest !
Ah, Life so sweet ! so fugitive !
Dear Mother, endless sleep is best,
But ere we close our eyes in rest
We loathe the Power which made us live.

" What mercy hast thou, Father ?   None,
Even for thine own Belovëd Son,
Who weeping sadly, drinking up
The poison of thy hemlock cup,
While the rude rocks and clouds were shaken,
And even thine angels sobbed in pain,
Cried, " Eloi, why am I forsaken ? "

And dying, sought thy Face in vain ! . .
Reveal that Face !—Uplift thy veil,
O God, and show thyself, that we
Who struggling upward faint and fail
　May know thy lineaments and Thee !
Thou *canst* not, for thou *art* not !—I
Have never found in sea or sky
One living token that thou art,
One semblance of a Father's heart,
One look, one touch to attest thy claim
To godhead and a Father's name ! "

Bright crimson was the blood wherein
Those words were written down !

　　　　　　　" My sin
Falls like a garment to my feet,
Naked I front thy Judgment Seat,
Veil'd Maker of the World.　Thy Word
Breath'd on the darkness, and it stirred
And lived—for *what ?*　That Man might rise
With hopeless heaven-searching eyes,
Clothed in Thy likeness ?　*Thine?*—the Form
　No man hath seen, no man may know,
A Phantom riding on the Storm
　While Earthquake rends the earth below ;
While like a hawk that hunts its prey

Death, creeping on from plain to plain,
Tortures the Human night and day,
Wounds what 'twere pitiful to slay,
    And scatters Pestilence and Pain.
I tell thee, one poor human thing,
    One little suffering lamb, one frail
Form of thy cruel fashioning,
    Refutes the Lie which cries ' All Hail
Father Almighty ! '

                    " Mighty ?   No !
Weaker than we who come and go
Erect and proud, whose deeds approve
A human brotherhood of love.
Our love and hate have aims, but thine
    Are idle bolts at random hurl'd,
Impotent, hidden, yet Divine,
    Brood o'er thy broken-hearted World ! "

My last quotation (for the present)
Though far less fierce, is still unpleasant :

" *Pictor Ignotus !* Power Unseen !
    Who limn'd this sight whereon I gaze,—
The still blue Seas, the arc serene
Of yon still Heavens of radiant sheen,
    I doff my hat and give Thee praise !

Thy skill in painting this green Earth,
    The forms upright that seem divine,
Proclaim Thy most exceeding worth—
    No *technique*, Master, equals Thine !
Step forward, then, O great Unknown,
    Accept our humble admiration !—
All men of taste will gladly own
    The excellence of Thy Creation !
A beauteous bit of work like *this*
    Whereon I feast mine eyes this morning,
All peace, all prettiness, all bliss,
    Hushes at once all doubt, all scorning.
Tell me, Great Master, did'st Thou make
This thing for the mere Beauty's sake,
Having no other test to measure
Thy work, but pure æsthetic pleasure ?
If this be so, why do we see
Elsewhere, attributed to Thee,
So many things which, I opine,
Are really coarse and Philistine ?
Another question, which concerns
    The æsthetic spirit.   Many hold,
However bright and clear it burns,
    'Tis selfish, passionless, and cold ;
Indifferent to the means whereby
    It gains the artistic end in view,
It broods alone, with cruel eye

That keeps the handcraft sure and true.
If this be so, and Thou, O great
    Master, art but a craftsman fine,
I understand and estimate
    (At last) Thy process, called " Divine "—
Cold to the prayer of human sorrow,
    Deaf to the sob of human strife,
Thou workest grandly, night and morrow,
    On Thy great Masterpiece of Life !
For Thine own pleasure is it done,
    Since Art's delight is in the doing,
Thine own enjoyment, slowly won,
    Is the sole end Thou art pursuing—
No dull despairing criticaster
Troubles Thee or disturbs Thee, Master !
No thought of human approbation
Perturbs Thy rapture of Creation !
No sound of breaking hearts can reach Thee,
    No touch of tears Thy sense can thrill,
Tho' millions praise Thee or beseech Thee,
    Indifferent Thou labourest still ;
Picture on Picture is destroyed,
And thrown into the empty void ;
World upon world is made, and then
Rejected gloomily again ;
Life upon life is painted fair,
Then tost aside in Art's despair ;

And so, with blunders infinite,
Thou toilest for Thine own delight !

" And when Thy task is done, when Art
    Crowns to the full Thy great endeavour,
Alone, Unknown, still sit apart,
    And glory in Thy work for ever ! "—

V.

There, where eternal Summer lingers,
  The Isle lay golden 'neath the blue,
Save when the Rain's soft tremulous fingers
  Just touch'd its eyes with cool dark dew,—
Or when with sudden thunderous cry
The chariots of the clouds went by,
And trembling for a little space,
The Isle lay down with darken'd face
Under the vials of the Storm,
  Then shook the sparkling drops away
And looking upward felt the warm
  New sunlight gladdening thro' the grey !
Like a child's heart that beats so gladly,
  So full of joy for Life's own sake,
Did not the sudden tears flow madly
  A moment's space, 'twould surely break,—
So did that Land of Summer capture,
Just now and then surcease from rapture !
But after storms, the bliss grew finer,
  And storms indeed were far between,—
The days divine, the nights diviner,
  With peace celestial and serene.

From dawn to dark the golden Light
Dwelt on green cape and gleaming height,

I

On yellow sands where the blue Sea
Pencil'd in silvern filagree
Frail flowers and leaves of frost-white spray
That ever came and flash'd away.
Then, the deep nights! great nights of calm,
Full of ambrosial bliss and balm!
Smooth sun-stain'd waves as daylight fled
Broke on the reef to foam blood-red,
Till the white Moon arose, and lo!
The foam was powdery silver snow,
And slowly, softly, down the night,
   O'er the smooth black and glistering Sea,
The starry urns of crystal Light
   Were fill'd and emptied momently!
Then in the centre of the glimmer
   The round Moon ripen'd as she rose,
And cover'd with the milk-white shimmer
   The glassy Waters took repose ;
And round the Isle a murmur deep
Of troubled surges half asleep
Broke faintlier and faintlier
   As Midnight took her shadowy throne ;
In heaven, on earth, no breath, no stir,
   No sound, save that deep slumb'rous tone!
Wonder of Darkness !—'neath its wing
All living things sank slumbering,
Save those glad lovers in delight
   Clinging and gazing at the sky,

While phosphorescent thro' the night
   Portents of Nature glimmer'd by !
In such dark hours of stillness Love
   Reaches her apogee of bliss ;
The fountains of the spirit move
   Upward, and cresting to a kiss
Sink earthward sighing—then we seem
Creatures of passion and of dream,
Ethereal shadowy things whose breath
May touch the cheeks of happy Death,
Who smile, and sigh for joy, and fall
Into deep rest celestial !

Such joy I've had on autumn eves
When the Moon shines on slanted sheaves,
And thro' the distant farm-house pane
   The lighted candle flashes red,
And darker over field and lane
   The gloaming of the night is shed.
Then, pillow'd on a warm white breast,
   And gazing into happy eyes,
While the faint flush of radiance blest
   Still came and went on the dark skies,
I've felt the dim Earth softly spinning
   On its smooth axle, while above
The bright stars as at Time's beginning
   Turn'd, in their spheres of Light and Love ;—
O joy of Youth ! O adumbration

Of Hope and ecstasy intense!
When Life's faint stir, Love's first pulsation,
   Turn to a splendour dazzling sense!
One night like that were more to me,
   Now I am weary with Earth's ways,
Than all a long Eternity
   Of strident, garish, gladsome days!
Ah, to be young! ah, once again
   To drink Youth's wild and wondrous wine!
To quit the pathos and the pain
   For passionate hours of joy divine!
To feel the breast that comes and goes
   While fond white arms around me twine,
To feel the ripe mouth like a rose
   Prest close, with kiss on kiss, to mine!
To feel all Nature thus fulfil
   Her gladness in that touch of lips,
Which cling and cling and cling, and thrill
   One Soul to the soft finger-tips,—
All this, which I can ne'er express,
This flush of Youth and Happiness,
Methinks is infinitely nicer
   Than being counted good or clever—
Than growing every day preciser
   And finding Love has flown for ever!
For ever? No!—Thank God, the power
Of Love can move me to this hour;
And tho' my moonlight pranks are over,

And those old sheaves are shed like sleet,
I'll be a Poet and a Lover
Until my heart doth cease to beat!

Yet there are nobler things than pleasure,
    Diviner things than Flesh can gain,—
Insight too deep for joy to measure
    Comes with supremacy of pain !—
When kneeling by the Dead and seeing
    That still white Lily with shut eyes,
We feel, stirred to the depths of Being,
    The pathos of poor human ties.
If in that awful trysting place,
    We watch, thro' tears that blindly roll,
Pale Love and shadowy Death embrace
    And blend to one eternal Soul,
How feeble, of how little worth,
Seem all those ecstasies of Earth !
Out of corruption and decay
Spring flowers that cannot pass away—
Out of a grief transcending tears
    Springs radiance that redeems our lot,
While faintly on our listening ears
Rings the soft music of the spheres,
    ' Forget me not ! forget me not ! '
Shall we forget ?   Shall Death not be
The gauge of our Humanity ?
Shall Love and Death, one Soul, one Thought,

Not waft us upward as on wings ?
Almighty God, our life were nought,
Were this dark Miracle ne'er wrought
    To prove us spiritual things.
Dust to the dust—there let it die !
Soul to the Soul—which cannot die !
The dim white Dove of Death is winging
    O'er Life's great flood in lonely flight,
That sad black leaf of olive bringing
    To prove a hidden Land of Light !
God, who created Earth and Heaven,
    Lord of the Dead thy love can save,
Thy Bow still comforts the bereaven
    While Death wings on from wave to wave !
Standing 'neath Sorrow's sunless pall
    We hail a symbol bright and blest,
And by that sign know one and all
That when these troubled Waters fall
    Our Ark on Ararat shall rest ! . . . .

So the sweet days stole on, and still
The Outcast wandered at his will
From dream to dream, from bliss to bliss,
    Glad and unconscious of his doom ;
His thought, a smile—his life, a kiss—
    His breath and being, one perfume !

But even as the Snake once stole

Unseen, unguess'd, to Eden's Bowers,
Ennui, the Serpent of the Soul,
   Crept in deep-hid 'neath fruit and flowers!
Slowly the ecstasy intense
Fever'd the life of Soul and Sense,
And certain of delight the eyes
Grew weary of the happy Skies.
And looking up into his face,
Her only Heaven, the Maid could trace,
Ere he himself was yet aware,
The filmy clouds of nameless care!
Sometimes he'd sit wrapt deep in thought,
   His gaze upon the glassy Sea;
Sometimes from sleep his passion-fraught
   Spirit would wake him suddenly!
Sometimes, on days of summer rain,
   When gentle storms swept round the land,
He paced the shores, and seemed again
   Upon the wave-tost deck to stand!
And wistful as a hound, that lies
Watching its master's face, and tries
To share his sorrow or delight,
The Maiden mark'd him day and night!

" This is the worst of Joy—the more
   We bask (he writes) beneath its ray,
The sooner is the magic o'er,
   The quicklier doth it fade away!

Sunshine without a cloud at all
Of its own peace begins to pall,
And calm too tropic and intense
Soon fevers to indifference !
Whence little rain-clouds, tempests even,
  Keep Hymen's garden green and growing,
And lovers weary of a Heaven
  Where no rain falls, no wind is blowing !
One sickens of fine weather, tires
Of ever-gratified desires,
Is bored, although at first enchanted,
By having every fancy granted.
And ah ! my little Maid, unskill'd
  In any art of the coquette,
All love, all rapture, sweetly filled
With the warm wine her soul distilled,
  Incapable of fear or fret,
Ne'er knew what women more capricious
  Learn, with long culture for a guide,—
That joy is render'd more delicious
  By being now and then denied.
How could a Passion-Flower, all scent,
All bloom, and all abandonment,
Appreciate the subtle ways
  Which wiser modern women show forth ?
Such dainty tricks came in with stays,
  Flounces, and pantalettes, and so forth,—
Whence we our Modern Venus see,

Not in immortal nudity,
But veil'd in beauteous mystery !
But Love in that bright Land abode
    Almost in mother-nakedness,
Pure Nature all her beauties showed
    Indifferent to the arts of Dress :
No Milliner had wander'd thither,
Bearing Parisian magic with her :—
The skirt's sly folds, the robe's disguises,
    The pruderies of silken hose,
The roguish petticoat's surprises,
The thousand spells that Art devises
    To veil the secrets of the Rose !
That Child of Sunlight never guess'd
    How winsome and how fair may be
A modern Maiden bravely drest
    In opalescent modesty !
The scented form that shrinks away
    At the first look of tenderness,
The faltering tongue that murmurs 'nay,'
    Belying eyes that answer ' yes,'
The flying feet a lover chases,
    The half-withdrawn, half-lingering hand,
The breast that heaves 'neath creamy laces
Craving yet shrinking from embraces,
    Were all unknown in that sweet Land ! "

And so, already, as I've told,

The fabled Snake was crawling there,
Since he who trod those shores of gold
    Had brought it with him unaware !—
For worldly knowledge and its pride
    Tainted the man's dark nature thro',
And as they wandered side by side,
Lonely as Adam and his Bride,
    Under those skies of Eden's blue,
He often watched her in the mood
    Of modern Bards and Heroes, saying :
' True, she is beautiful and good,
As fine a thing of flesh and blood
    As ever loved or went a-Maying.
She recognises, too, completely
    The privilege of her master Man,
And, ever fond and smiling sweetly,
    Supplies his needs, as Woman can.
She is the instrument placed by me
To calm, perhaps to purify, me !
And I, of course, in this affair,
Fit object of her daily prayer,
Am the one person whose salvation
God takes into consideration !
I am the Hero—I am clearly
    The object of His circumspection,
And *she*, although I love her dearly,
    Is but a means to my perfection.'
And so, like other cultivated

Dunces by Folly sublimated,
He took that angel's fond and true
Homage as if it were his due !
A Hero !—*he ?*   Now God confound him,
   And all such Heroes great or small—
The crown of pride with which Love crown'd him
   Was but a Fool's cap after all !

VI

Heroes ?   The noblest and the best
    Are those of whom we never know ;
God's Greatest are God's Lowliest,
Who move unnoted to their rest
    Nor build their pride on human woe.
Napoleons of Sword or Song,
The proud, the radiant, and the strong,
The inheritors of Earth, are clay
To the slain Saints of every day.
The Kings of Action and of Thought,
    Pass in their pride and leave no sign,
But the slain Martyr's flesh is wrought
    By suffering to Life divine.
In the eternal Judge's sight
    This truth refutes the common lie :
What men call Genius hath no right
    To scorn one single human tie.

Come up, ye Poets, and be tried !
    Stand up, you shrieking, mouthing throng !
Shall *you* be spared and justified
    For a few scraps of selfish song ?
By Heaven, the weary world could spare
    All poets since Creation's day,

If one poor human heart's despair,
One poor lost Soul's unheeded prayer,
   Must be the price it hath to pay !
Bury your Homers mountain-deep,
   Strangle your Shakespeares ere they wake,
If they their heritage must keep,
If they Parnassus-ward must creep
   O'er souls they stain and hearts they break.
For what is Verse, and what is Fame ?
Great reams of paper, much acclaim !
And what are Poets at the best
   But busy tongues that often bore us ;
One noble heart, one loving breast
   Is worth the whole long-winded chorus !

But hold ! true Poesy keeps ever
   Great wisdom as its pearl of price ;
The sleepless Dream, the long Endeavour,
The questioning Thought that resteth never,
   Demand no living sacrifice.
Your Goethe's pyramid was made
Of broken hearts and lives betrayed,
Wherefore men found it, when complete,
A pyramid of Self-conceit.
And take your Shelley (tho' I hold
The fellow had a harp of gold) :
He stained the Soul he had to save
The day he turn'd from Harriet's grave.

But leave me Burns, and Byron too,—
They had their faults, and those not few,
And gave the nations much offence
By riot and concupiscence,
But Love was in the rogues! they paid
Full dearly for the pranks they played,
And never, in their wildest revel,
   Pleaded the *privilege* of Fame,
Or called on Genius and the Devil
   To *justify* their guilt and shame!

Some men, all women, worship Strength :
   Carlyle did, till experience taught him
That even the athlete pays at length
   The bills that Time and Death have brought him.
Rough Thomas loudly preached for long
That hero-worship of the Strong,
The right of muscle and of sinew
   To use the weak and crush the small.
' Do something! show the spirit in you,
   Work, in God's name!' men heard him call.
' Speech, sirs, is silvern—silence gold !'
   He cried aloud with lungs of leather ;
Nay, even when wearied out and old
   He could not keep his tongue in tether.
Friedrich, Napoleon, Mirabeau,
   Danton and Goethe, were his crazes !
They stood like puppets in a row,

Tall spectres of a wax-work show,
    While lustily he shrieked their praises.
Meantime the bleeding Christ went by,
    And heard the acclaim in Cheyne Walk,
Heard from the threshold, with a sigh,
    The creed of Silence proved by Talk,
And passing slowly on, footsore,
Left on the noisy Prophet's door
The mark of Passover, for token
A Lamb must die, a life be broken.
'Twas done, and in a little space,
    Silent at last as in a tomb,
The Prophet, tears on his worn face,
    Sat old and lonely in the gloom.
How did his Heroes help him then ?
    What word had Friedrich, Mirabeau,
Napoleon, and the mighty men
He glorified with tongue and pen,
    To assuage the tempest of his woe ?
Old Hurricane, I hated thee
When, shrieking down Humanity,
    High as a Dervish thou upleapt,—
But in thine hour of agony,
    I could have kissed thy wounds and wept.
The pity ! ah, the pity of it !
    Well, Life is piteous at the best.
Thou wast most mighty, poor old Prophet,
    When weakest, saddest, silentest !

Tho' all the gods were dead, and He,
The great God, who is One in Three,
" *Did* ought " (at least in thy opinion,
    Though thou did'st cry His Name so loud)
Though Belial reigned in His dominion
    And led the many-headed crowd,
Yet supernatural Shapes of Fear,
    Fiend-like or god-like, passed thee by,
And Froude, thy Nemesis, was near
    With watchful biographic eye.
Heir to thy weariness and folly,
    He warm'd thy night-cap, brought thy gruel,
Sat by thine arm-chair, melancholy,
    And fed thy fantasy with fuel.
And now across the earth he passes,
    Babbling of thee and Parson Lot,
And serves up tepid for the masses
    Thy gospel, once so piping hot ;
Feeds little strong men with his praise,
    Just as *you* fed the strong and great,
Bewails the dark degenerate days,
The dreadful Democratic craze,
    The shipwreck of our ancient State ;
Longs for another Drake (or gander),
    Of whom in Eyre he saw some traces,
Some rough, swashbuckler, bold commander,
    To govern the inferior races ;

Thro' the colonial seas careering
Avers philanthropies are vile,
And rests, forlornly pamphleteering,
The Peter Patter of Carlyle.

Man is most godlike, I affirm,
Not when he seeks to top the skies,
And peer, poor evanescent Worm,
Into the heavenly Sphynx's eyes,
Not when he vainly tries to patter
Of Gods and heroes, Mind and Matter,
Or cries, with folly sublimated,
"Lo, I am first of things created,"
Or flapping further leaden-bodied
Assumes a legislative godhead;—
But when, in tears, he humbly kneeling
Prays in the silence of the night,
Knows himself blind, and dimly feeling
With frail arms upward, craves for Light!
Then, from without or from within,
Comes in that solemn silent hour
The miracle which turns his sin
To hope, to insight, and to power!
Then comes the Voice from far away,
Saying—' My love shall be thy guerdon!
Be of good heart, poor thing of clay,
Soon shall I turn thy night to day,
And free thy Soul from flesh, its burden!

K

He listens, breaks to tears, and. straightway
   Feels this rough load of bone and brawn
Grow lighter, sees a heavenly Gateway
   Swing on its hinges far withdrawn,
Revealing glimpses bright and blest
   Of good old-fashion'd Realms of Rest,—
The Heaven which all his kin have sighed for,
   Which bards have dream'd of, martyrs died for,
Which Christ the Master postulated,
   Which every creed hath pictured *there*,
Which Death itself hath adumbrated
   Out of the cloud of Life's despair !

Dear foolish Creed ! sweet Superstition !
   Fair childish Dream, now faded wholly !
By men of brains and erudition
   Despised as ignorance and folly !
Humanity, the wise inform us,
   Is intellectual, or nought,
And Heroes, wondrous and enormous,
   Have soared to thrones of godlike thought,
Attesting that Humanity
By its own seed redeemed may be,
And that the Titans of each nation
May face the Saturn of Creation.
For " God "—if there be God at all—
   Does nothing (that's the Chelsea teaching !)
And to be weak and frail and small,
To reach up arms and feebly call

On some veil'd Nurse, in blind beseeching,
Is just to forfeit altogether
    The privilege of Adam's seed!—
"No, if in Nature's stormy weather,
    You'd find a foothold and a creed,
A light, a buckler, an example,
    A sign to swear by (or to swear at),
Find out some Hero strong and ample
Who on your neck hath strength to trample,
    Crying, ' *Qui meruit palmam ferat !* '
Follow that form the small birds sing to,
O'er fields of slain the vultures wing to,
    While women wail and warriors revel !
Since you can find no God to cling to,
    Worship some proud heroic Devil !" . . .

Well, to my Tale—for I'm digressing
Most damnably, and space is pressing.

At times, indeed, despite the curse
    Of Knowledge in him, *my* poor Hero,
Lord of his own Soul's universe,
    Yet lone as Lapland, low as zero,
Felt childishly beatified,
    Foolishly pious, tried to gulp a
Tear of repentance down, and cried—
"Lord of the meek, forgive my pride,
    O *mea culpa ! mea culpa !* "

For even a Hero, one who deems
 Himself the centre of Creation,
Who, proud of God's attention, beams
 With self-approving admiration,
Is only clay! A great philosopher
 Will often whimper on the sly,
And sceptics often try to cross over
 The Bridge of Prayers that spans the Sky.
On moonlight nights, on Sabbath days,
When Earth herself lies still and prays
Rock'd in the sad Sea's quiv'ring arms,
 And God's Hand, laid upon her breast,
Mid folds of trembling darkness, charms
 Her fears to momentary rest,
All creatures, proud or lowly, share
That dusky rapture of despair!
And now the Outcast who had sneer'd
 At all the schemes of Earth and Heaven,
Who fear'd no wrath or tempest, feared
 The peace, the joy, which God had given!
And gazing in that Maiden's eyes
Full of soft love and sad surmise,
He saw a starry radiance shine
That show'd *him* base, and *her* divine!
Ah, then he could have prayed, and wept,
 Humble, and low, and spirit-sore—
But the mood past, and o'er him crept
 The cankering curse of pride once more.

" Sometimes upon the peaceful Sea
They paddled out."—*Page* 149.

Yet those were happy, happy days !
'Twas Eden, tho' the Snake was there !
Eternal Summer shed its rays
O'er these still seas, thro' these green ways,
    And all was primitive and fair !
Life grew so still and softly sweet
The rapturous heart scarce seem'd to beat,
And sense and spirit seem'd to swoon
To the hot hush of one long Noon !
Sometimes thro' forest paths of green
They walk'd, and thro' the leafy sheen
O'erhead, beheld the bright skies grow
Miraculously white, like snow ;
Or to some grotto's shade they came
    And saw with slimy weeds o'ergrown
Some carven god without a name
    Sit in the chillness all alone,
And on her face the little Maid
Fell for a space and softly prayed,
Then dipt her finger tips into
The cool green drops of sunless dew
That on the idol dript and fell,
    And laid them on her lover's brow,
And seem'd to say, ' Love, all is well—
    He gives us both his blessing *now !* '
Sometimes upon the peaceful Sea
    They paddled out in light canoes,
And floating softly, silently,

O'er deep cool voids of rainbow hues,
Saw far below them, far as was
The mirror'd heaven as smooth as glass,
Thro' soft translucent depths of dream,
    Down, down, within the clear abysm,
Bright creatures of the Ocean gleam
    And fade, like colours in the prism ;—
There, rock'd on crystal waves that were
As clear and shadowless as air,
They seem'd suspended near the sun
Between two Heavens that throb'd as one!
Sometimes they climb'd the peaks, and stood
Full in the moonlight's amber flood,
And saw the great stars bright as gold
Steal breathless from the azure fold,
And like strange luminous living things
More to their silent pasturings ;
And down beneath them, far as gaze
Could see into the ocean-ways,
Such shapes as in a mirror shone,
And softly pasturing too, crept on !
And all around them on the heights
Eternity set beacon-lights,
And meteors, flashing suddenly,
Fell radiant from sky to sea,
While sadly as some heart bereaven
Throb'd the great luminous Heart of Heaven !

Almighty God, who out of clay
Fashioned us creatures of a day,
Who gave us vision to perceive,
And souls to wonder and believe,
How calmly, coldly, we behold
Thy daily marvels manifold !
Thy raiment-hem of glory sweeps
Across the darkness of the Deeps,
And quickens light and life, O God,
In all it touches, stone or clod—
And we . . . things of a day, an hour.
Accept the wonder as our dower,
And wearying of the splendour, lust
For darkening pleasures of the dust.
Tho' thou hast girdled us around
With ecstacies of sight and sound,
Tho' all without us and within
    Thy Thought takes form and adumbration,
Dark is the answer it doth win
    From us, the waifs of thy creation !
We cry for Miracles; and lo !
    All Nature is illumed for us !
The sun, the stars, the flowers, the snow,
    Change at thy touch miraculous—
In vain, in vain, the Mystery,
We understand not, tho' we see,
And like sick children, turning thence,
Fret out our little sum of sense !

Yet sometimes to thy touch we quicken
A moment, like that Man and Maiden,—
And while thy wonders round us thicken
We pause and marvel, passion-laden,—
Then lifted in some air divine
   High o'er this world to yonder Sky,
See, where thy constellations shine,
   The Darkness of thy Face go by !
An instant only !—could the wonder
   Last but another, then indeed
Our bonds of flesh were torn asunder,
   And we were purified and freed—
But no !—the thrill celestial
Ceases, and down to Earth we fall,
And coldly once again survey
Thy miracles of Night and Day !

Back to our lovers !   Could I tell
   Of all they felt and dream'd and thought,
How Love for ever changed the spell
   That bound their spirits fever-fraught,
How night and day their lives were blent
In rapture and abandonment,
My song would never end !—the Hours
Flew by like maidens crown'd with flowers,
Each like the other dancing on,
Till many nights and days were gone.
How many—who can tell ?   Not I—

For in these passionate relations,
We count not Time as it goes by,
But measure it by palpitations :
At last, we waken, and look back
Along the pleasant flowery track
By which we've journey'd, and discover
The flowers are flown, the leaves are dead ;—
So, at least, was it with our Lover,
When his long honeymoon was over
And the first bloom of Love had fled.
And how it would have ended, whether
He would have stealthily departed,
Or roughly cut the tender tether
That held their sunny lives together,
And left the maiden broken-hearted,
I know not. Fate, the wild Witch-woman
Who thwarts the plans of all things human,
Came flying to that Isle so sunny
With imps of mischief in her train,
And changed Love's waning moon of honey
Into a baleful star of pain !

VII.

Beneath thick boughs of emerald green
  Turn'd by the sunlight's golden ray
To curtains of transparent sheen,
  They had roam'd, for half a summer's day:
Now resting in the dappled shade
  By silvern fount or bubbling well,
Now passing thro' some open glade
  Where the spent shafts of splendour fell;
But ever as they wander'd on
  The man look'd dark as one who dreams,
With inward-looking eyes that shone
  To restless melancholy gleams;
And all her loving arts were vain
To stir the shadow of this pain;
On passive lips as chill as clay
Her kisses fell; her warm hand lay
Fluttering in a hand of stone;
No look of love, no tender tone,
Answer'd the sweetness of her own;
Till suddenly the umbrage deep
Of those great woodlands still as sleep
Parted, and grassy heights were gained
Sloping to great crags crimson-stain'd,
And 'tween the crags, that heavenward rose
  Crown'd with one solitary palm,

The Ocean !—troublous in repose,
Murmurous in folds of summer calm !

Then his eye brighten'd, and with fleet
Footsteps he hasten'd on until,
Where the high cliffs and clouds did meet,
The white surge far beneath his feet,
    He paused, and gladdening drank his fill
Of some new rapture.   Blithe and bright,
    To see his gloom had passed away,
She join'd him on the lonely height,
    And, happy as a child at play,
Ran gathering ferns and flowers that grew
Above the chasm's purple blue
Between her and the rocky shore ;—
    She scarce could hear so far away
The breaking billows' ceaseless roar,
    But saw the line of snow-white spray
Frozen by distance.   Then she turn'd,
And lo ! his face no longer yearn'd
Fondly to hers, but eagerly
Bent to the far-off shoreless Sea !
And ah ! the hunger and the thirst
Of sleepless wanderers tempest-nurst,
The look which wives and mothers fear
I' the eyes of those they hold so dear,
The rapture which is Love's despair,
The unrest of Ocean, all were there,

Mirror'd in that bright restless gaze
Which swept the wondrous watery ways !

She spoke—he smiled !—and she could read
In that strange smile the doom of Love !
No more her own, in dream or deed,
    Lifted in some wild air above
Her hopes and dreams, he felt again
The power, the passion, and the pain
Of that Revolt, that mad Surmise,
The sleepless Waters symbolize !
But then he looked at her and smiled
    Again,—and now it seemed once more
The smile of Love, tho' wan and wild,
    Not soft and sunny as before ;
And gazing back thro' tender tears
    She drank the smile, and softly scan'd
Her lover's face, while on her ears
    Fell words she could not understand.

' Close to me, close ! ' he cried aloud,
    ' Would that this hour, my child, we twain
Might mingle, drifting like one cloud
    Over the melancholy Main !
Would that the cup thy love hath brought
    Might quench the thirst of my despair !
Would that my spirit fever-fraught
    Might kneel with thine in peaceful prayer !

But no, the golden Dream is done,
    (O God, how sweet ! O God, how fair !)
Thy life grows here beneath the sun,
    Mine is among the Storms, out there !
God bless thee, child—if God there be,
    His benediction *must* be thine—
But voices yonder from the Sea,
    Voices of Souls as lost as mine,
Still call aloud that He I name
Hath still no power to calm or tame
The spirit who denies and spurns
The peace for which thy nature yearns.
The storm-cloud touches with its shower
    The flower that blossoms sweet and low—
But the cloud blends not with the flower,
    Nor rests in peace where flowers may grow.
My child, my child ! Would I had been
    Pure like thyself and purely true,
Sure of my dower of Light serene,
    Sure of the earth from which I grew—
But no ! no rest, no joy, contents
    The outcast Soul, the sleepless Will—
And what the cruel Elements
    Have mixed in wrath, no Love can still ! '

Even as a child who tries to guess
    The words she little understands,
But kindles into happiness

Thro' smile of eyes and clasp of hands,
She listened! then her lips to his
Were sealèd in a heavenly kiss,
And running from his side again
   She gathered flowers and brought them to him,
And as he took them, piteous pain,
   Scornful yet wistful, trembled thro' him.
As some bright bird of Paradise,
   Or some fair fawn-like pard, seem'd she,
An earthly thing with elfin eyes,
   Scarce humanized, yet fond and free;
And lo, he loved her,—as men love
   Earth and the flowers that blossom thence,
The beasts and birds of wood and grove,
All happy things that live and move
   Like apparitions round the sense;
But deep within his troubled breast
An alien love, a vague unrest,
Stirr'd to a sense of vaster things,
   Great doubts and dreams, divine desire,—
An eagle's thirst to unfold its wings,
Upward to fly in circling rings
   And front the blinding solar fire!

High o'er the utmost crag there grew
   The palm-tree, rooted in the rock,
Bent by each ocean-blast that blew
   But firm amidst the tempest's shock,

And round its roots, beneath its shade,
   Flowers like our wind-flower clustering crept,—
Thither, swift-footed, unafraid,
   Laughing, the little Maiden leapt ;
Till down beneath her fairy feet
She saw the distant surges beat,—
Great birds that look'd like butterflies
   Hovering white o'er ridgéd waves,
While trumpet-calls and thunder-cries
   Rose from the distant chasms and caves ;—
Then as she gained the lonely tree,
   And stooped among the flowers, the sound
Of air and water suddenly
   Thunder'd like earthquake all around !
Fearless and happy, white and fair,
She paused in pretty wonder there,
Then looking back beheld her lover
   Beckoning with face as pale as death.
' Come back, come back ! ' he cried, while over
   The gulf she hung with bated breath—
Then smiling back to him who yearn'd
Beyond her, merrily she turn'd,
And kneeling o'er the chasm hung
To pluck one fair white flower that clung
Beneath her o'er the chasm's gloom,
With light quick finger touch'd the bloom,
And *then* . . .
          Great God, who gav'st us sight,

Yet see'st us grope with close-shut eyes,
Blind to the blessings of the Light,
Dead to the Love that deifies !
Unto how many men each hour
    Frail little fingers seek to bring
Some gentle gift of love, some flower
    That is the Soul's best offering ?
Some happiness which we despise,
    Some boon we toss aside for ever,—
And only that our selfish eyes
    May smile one moment on the giver !
How many of us count or treasure
    The little lives that perish thus,
To garner us a moment's pleasure,
    A moment's space to comfort us ?
Blind, ever blind, we front the sun
    And cannot see the angels near us,
Forget the tender duties done
    By willing slaves, to help and cheer us !
Earth and its fulness, all the fair
Creations of this heaven and air,
All lives which die that we may live,
    All gifts of service, we pass by,
All blessings Love hath power to give
    We scorn, O God, or we deny !
Is there a man beneath the sun,
    Tho' poor and basest of the base,
For whom such duty is not done

" A still white form stretch'd silently
On thoso cold rocks that fringed the Sea ! "—*Page* 161.

To pleasure him a little space ?
A singing bird, a faithful hound,
A loving woman, or a child,
Contented with our voice's sound
Patient in death if *we* have smiled,
These, these, O God, are daily sent
To give thine outcasts sacrament,
And in so giving themselves attain
Thy sacred privilege of pain !
Yet still our eyes turn sunward blindly,
And blindly still our souls contemn
The loving hands that touch us kindly,
The lips that kiss our raiment's hem ;
And we forget or turn away
From flowers that blossom on our way ;
Blind to the gentle ministration
Of tutelary angels near,
We find too late that our salvation
Lies near, not far ;—not there, but *here !* .

Even then, as with her little hand
She grasped the flower and sought to rise,
The crag's edge crumbled into sand,
And fluttering from her lover's eyes
She vanished !—With a shriek of dread
He gained the crag, and pausing there,
The great rocks trembling neath his tread,
Gazed down—and down—thro' voids of air,

L

And saw beneath him, thro' the snow
Of flying foam that rose below,
A still white form stretch'd silently
On those cold rocks that fringed the Sea!
What next did pass, he knew not.   When
His blinded soul grew clear again,
He stood beneath the craggy height
Close to the surges flashing white,
And, dazzled by the foam and spray,
     Bent o'er that bruised and bleeding Form;—
Crush'd on the cruel shore it lay,
     Silent and still, yet soft and warm;
And as he knelt with tender cries
     Lifting her gently to his breast,
She stir'd and moan'd,—then, opening eyes,
     With one last smile serene and blest,
Brighten'd to see her Master bow
     Above her, gladly drank his breath,
With fluttering fingers smooth'd his brow,
     Kiss'd him, and closed her eyes in death!

How still it was! the clouds above
Paused quietly and did not move—
The waves lay down like lambs—the sound
Of crags and waves was hushed all round.
' O God, my God!' the Outcast said,
Kissing the lips still warm and red,
While the frail form hung lax and dead.

And lo ! there stole upon his ear,
Low as his own heart's beat, yet clear,
A murmur faint as Sabbath bells
Heard far away mid forest dells
Buried in leaves and haze, so still
And soft it only seems the thrill
Of silence thro' the summer air—
A sigh of rapture and of prayer !

And lo ! his dark face seaward turn'd,
As in a vision he discerned,
    Thro' thickly flowing tears, a Form
In saffron robes and golden hair,
Walking with rosy feet all bare
    The Waters slumbering after storm !

A Maiden Shape, her sad blue eyes
Soft with the peace of Paradise,
She walked the waves ; in her white hand
Pure lilies of the Heavenly Land
Hung alabaster white, and all
The billows neath her light footfall
Heaved glassy still, and round her head
    An aureole burnt of golden flame,
As nearer yet, with radiant tread,
    Fixing her eyes on his, she came.
Then as she paused upon the Sea
Gazing upon him silently

With looks insufferably bright
　And gentle brows beatified,
He knew our Lady of the Light,
　Mary Madonna, heavenly-eyed !

He look'd—he listen'd.
　　　　　　　　　　'Speak !' she said,
' By Him who judgeth quick and dead,
Art thou content for evermore
　Here on the lotus leaf to rest ?
Speak ! and thy wanderings are o'er,
　And sleep is thine—if sleep be best !
Speak ! and this fluttering flower of flesh
Shall lift its head and bloom afresh,
Guide and companion unto thee
Thro' Eden for Eternity ;—
She loves thee, as the birds and flowers
　Love, and all things of sun and shore.
Speak !—and the sunshine and the showers
Shall lap thee deep in these bright bowers
　For ever and for evermore.'
He answer'd, heavy-eyed and pale,
　' Madonna ! let me journey on !
Better the surges and the gale,
Better to sail and sail and sail
　Before thy wind, Euroclydon.
Here have I found delight and joy,
　Here hath my spirit been renew'd,

Yea, with the mad thirst of a boy,
  All Adam burning in my blood,
I have drunken of the brimming cup
Nature for ever holdeth up.
Nay more, the primal sympathy,
  The first sweet force which stirs thro' all,
Hath quicken'd gentler thoughts in me
  Than yonder where the Tempests call—
Deep pity kindles in my heart
  For all glad things beneath the Blue,
For her, the brightest and the best,
  This life of sunlight and of dew;
And yet . . . and yet . . . tho' I can weep
  Above her, since she loved me so,
I would not wake her from her sleep
  To share my happiness or woe !
Poor child, she knew no thought of pain !
  A blossom, born to bloom and kiss,
She open'd, then stole back again
  To Nature's elemental bliss !
Here let her dwell, till Time is done,
With all such creatures of the sun—
Here let her still remain, a part
Of Nature's warmly beating heart;—
Here, blest and blessing, wrapt up warm
  In kindling dust, her place shall be,
While I return to face the storm
  Out yonder on the sunless Sea ! "

Ev'n as he spake, the air grew dark,
 Some veil of awe shut out the day,
And voices from the Phantom Barque
 Cried, 'Hillo ! hillo ! come away !'
Then, while Our Lady's form grew dim
And vanish'd, with sad eyes on him,
He saw beyond the line of surge
 Breaking upon the lonely strand,
The shadow of the Ship emerge
 And hover darkly close to land.
And woeful voices of the Sea
Call'd to his soul tumultuously,
As kneeling by the Maiden's form
He kissed the lips that yet were warm,
And in the cold still ear that lay
 Frail as a little ocean-shell,
Once warm with life, then wash'd away,
 Whisper'd his passionate " farewell ! "
Then, moaning like a death-struck bird,
Sprang to his feet, and while he heard
The flapping sail, the whistling shroud,
 The murmuring voices, fill the gloom,
' I come ! I come !' he cried aloud,
 And totter'd to the Ship of Doom.

INTERLUDE.

INTERLUDE.

So endeth Song the First !
                Long years
Ere you and I, my love, were born,
The Outcast sail'd away, his ears
Full of mad music of the Morn.
Once more upon the lonely Main
He dree'd his weird of bitter pain,
Haunted by dreams where'er he flew
Of that sweet Child of sun and dew.
But ten years later, and every ten
At intervals 'twixt now and then,
He landed wearily again
And sought—what still he seeks in vain !
The record tells us of his quest
From north to south, from east to west,—
Affairs with most delightful ladies
    Of every clime beneath the sun,
From far Cathay to sunny Cadiz,
    From Ispahan to Patagon,—
Of all religions and complexions,
    Of every shape and every fashion ;
He learn'd all phases of affections,—
The dark sultana's introspections,
    The Persian concubine's soft passion !

Thus lightly roaming here and there,
  Seeking his fate from zone to zone,
Betimes he came to Weimar, where
  Jupiter-Goethe had his throne :
This stately Eros in court-breeches
  Deign'd with our Pilgrim to converse,
But bored him hugely with set speeches
  And pyramids of easy verse,—
Of which some solid blocks still stand
Amid Saharas of mere sand.
In Germany he spent a year
  Of wondrous love and strange probation—
What of that land of bores and beer
He thought, you in good time shall hear,
  If I survive for the narration.
Soon afterwards I find that he
Roam'd southward, into Italy,
And standing near St Peter's dome,
Was present at the sack of Rome.
Thence in due time he wander'd right on
  To Paris, where, some years ago,
He saw the garish lamps flash bright on
  The Second Empire's feverish Show—
A Fair by gaslight—booths resplendent,
  Bright-tinsel'd players promenading,
Street lamps with handsome corpses pendent,
  Couples beneath them gallopading,
Soldiers and journalists saluting,

Poets and naked harlots dancing,
Drums beating, panpipes tootletooting,
  State wizards gravely necromancing ;
And in the midst, the lewd and yellow
God to whom wooden Joss was fellow,—
Enwrapt in purple, painted piebald,
Cigar in mouth, lack-lustre-eyeball'd,
Imperial Cæsar Punchinello !

But now, alas ! I hesitate ·
  Before I venture forward, dreading
My Hero's own unhappy fate,—
The peoples' scorn, the critics' hate,
  For dark's the path my Muse is treading !
And this strange poem is compounded
  Of mixtures new to modern taste,
And Mr Stead may be astounded
  And think my gentle Muse unchaste.
Until we reach the journey's end,
  (*Finis coronat opus !*) many
May dream I purpose to offend
  With merest horseplay, like a zany !
Mine is a serious song, however,
  As you shall see in God's good time,
If life should crown my long endeavour,
And grant me courage to perséver
  Thro' this mad maze of rakish rhyme.

I who now sing have been for long .
The Ishmaël of modern Song,—
Wild, tatter'd, outcast, dusty, weary,
Hated by Jacob and his kin,
Driv'n to the desert dark and dreary,
A rebel and a Jacobin;
Treated with scorn and much impatience
By gentlemanly reputations,
And by the critics sober-witted
Disliked and boycotted, or pitied.
I asked for bread, and got instead of
The crust I sought, a curse or stone,—
And so, like greater bards you've read of,
I've roamed the wilderness alone.
But that's all o'er, since I abandon
The ground free Mountain Poets stand on,
And kneel to say my catechism
Before the arch-priests of Nepotism.
Henceforth I shall no more resemble
Poor Gulliver when caught in slumber,
Swarm'd over, prick'd, put all a tremble,
By lilliputians without number.
The *Saturday Review* in pride
Will throne me by great Henley's side,
The *Daily News* sound my *Te Deum*
Despite the Devil and *Athenæum*;
Tho' Watts may triple his innuendoes,
And Swinburne shriek in sharp crescendoes,

The merry Critics all will pat me,
The merry Bards bob smiling at me,
All Cockneydom with crowns of roses
Salute my last apotheosis !

For (let me whisper in your ear !)
Of Criticism I've now no fear,
Since, knowing that the press might cavil,
I've joined the Critics' Club—the *Savile !*
And standing pledged to say things pleasant
Of all my friends, from Lang to Besant,
With many others, not forgetting
 Our school-room classic, Stevenson,
I look for puffs, and praise, and petting,
 From my new brethren, every one.
A Muse with half an eye and knock-knees
Would thrive, thus countenanced by Cocknies ;
And mine, tho' tall, and straight, and strong,
 Blest with a Highland constitution,
Has led a hunted life for long
 Thro' Cockney hate and persecution.

And yet—a terror trembles through me,
They may blackball, and so undo, me !
In that case I must still continue
 A Bard that fights for his own hand :
Bold Muse, then, strengthen soul and sinew
 To brave the lilliputian band !

I smile, you see, and crack my jest,
Altho' my fate has not been funny!
Storm-tost, and weary, and opprest,
The busy Bee has done his best,
But gather'd very little honey!
My life has ever been among
The drones, in deucëd rainy weather,
I've hum'd to keep my heart up, sung
A song or two of the sweet heather,
Nay, I've been merry too, and tried,
As now, to put my gloom aside;
But ah! be sure the mirth I wear
Is but a mask to hide my care,
Since on my soul and on my page
Fall shadows of a sunless age,
And sadly, faintly, I prolong
A broken life with broken song.
As Rome was once, when faith was dead,
And all the gentle gods were fled,
As Rome was, ere on Death's black tree
Bloom'd the Blood-rose of Calvary,
As Rome was, wrapt in cruel strife
By black eclipse of faith and life,
So is our world to-day!—and lo!
A cloud of weariness and woe,
Dark presage of the Tempest near,
Fills the sad universe with fear.

And in this darkness of eclipse,
When Faith is dumb upon the lips,
Hope dead within the heart, I share
The Time's black birthright of despair;
Hear the shrill voice that cries aloud
 'The gods are fallen and still must fall!
King of the sepulchre and shroud,
 Death keeps his Witch's Festival!'

Hark! on the darkness rings again,
Poor human Nature's shriek of pain,
Answer'd by cruel sounds that prove
The Life of Hate, the Death of Love.
Now, since all tender awe hath fled,
Not only for the gods o'erhead,
But for the tutelary, tiny,
 Gods that our daily paths surround,
The kindly, innocent, sunshiny
 Spirits that mask as ape and hound,—
Since neither under nor above him
Man reverences the powers that love him,
What wonder if, instead of these
 Who brought him gifts of joy for token,
Man looking upward only sees
 A hideous Spectre of the Brocken,
And 'mid his hush of horror, hears
The torrent-sound of human tears?
The butcher'd woman's dying shriek,

The ribald's laugh, the ruffian's yell,
While strong men trample on the weak,
Proclaim the reign of Hate and Hell.
And in the lazar-halls of Art,
And in the shrines of Science, priests
Of the new Nescience brood apart,
Crying, 'Man's life is as the Beast's !
There is no goodness 'neath the sun—
The days of God and gods are done,
And o'er the godless Universe
Falls the last pessimistic curse ! '

Old friends, with whom in days less dark
I roam'd thro' green Bohemia's glades,
While ' tirra lirra ' sang the lark
And lovers listen'd in the shades,
When Life was young and Song was merry,
And Morals free, and Manners bold,
When poets whistled ' hey-down-derry,'
And toil'd for love in lieu of gold,
When on the road we trode together
Old honest hostels offered cheer,
And halting in the sunny weather
We gladden'd over pipes and beer,—
Where are you hiding now ? and where
Is the Bohemia of our playtime ?
Where are the heavens that once were fair,
And where the blossoms of the Maytime ?

The trees are lopt by social sawyers,
  The grass is gone, the ways asphalted,
Stone walls set up by ethic lawyers
  Replace the Stiles o'er which we vaulted!
See! with rapidity surprising,
  Thro' jerry-building ministrations,
Neat Literary Villas rising
  To shelter timid reputations;
Each with its garden and its gravel,
  Its little lawn right trimly shaven,
Its owner's name, quite clean, past cavil,
  Upon a brass plate neatly graven!

And lo! that all mankind may know it,
  We are respectable or nothing,
The Seer, the Painter, and the Poet
  Must go in fashionable clothing—
High jinks, all tumbling in the hay,
  All thoughts of pipes and beer, are chidden,
The girls who were so glad and gay
Must be content in hodden-gray,
  Nay, merry books must be forbidden.
And—*ecce signum!*—primly drest
  Here come the .Vigilance Committee,
Condemning Murger and the rest
  Because they may corrupt the City!
Vie de Bohème!—Life yearned for yet,
En pantalon, en chemisette—

M

Life free as sunshine and fresh air,
Now gets no hearing anywhere,
And o'er a world of knaves and fools
The Moral Jerry-builder rules.

Moral ?   By Heaven, I see beneath
That saintly mask, the eyes of Death,
The wrinkled cheek, the serpent's skin,
The shy Mephistophelian grin !
And where he wanders thro' the land
    The green grass withers 'neath his tread,
While those trim villas built on sand
    Crumble around the living-dead.
Under the region he controls
Sound of a sleeping Earthquake rolls,
And at the murmur of his voice
The Seven Deadly Sins rejoice !

Meantime, the Jerry Legislator,
    Throttling all natures broad and breezy,
Flaunts in the face of the Creator,
The good old-fashioned Heavenly Pater,
    This gospel—' *Providence Made Easy !* '
Proving all gods but myths and fiction,
    He treats man's feeble constitution
With moral drugs and civic friction,
    To *force* the work of Evolution ;
Shows ' Rights ' are merely superstition,

And Freedom simply *Laissez faire,*
And puts a ban and prohibition
    On Life that once was free as air.
Behold the scientific dullard,
    Cocksure of healing Nature's plight,
Turning Thought's prism many-coloured
    Into one common black and white,
Measures our stature, rules our reading,
    Tells us that *he* is God's successor,
And vows no man of decent breeding
    Would seek a wiser Intercessor.
For ' Rights ' read ' Mights,' aloud cries he,
    ' For Thought, Paternal Legislation,'
And substitutes for Liberty
    The pompous Beadles of the Nation.
Aye me, when half Man's race is run,
    The screech-owl Science, which began
By flapping blindly in the sun,
Huskily croaking, ' Night is done !
    Hark to the Chanticleer of Man ! "
Now goose-like hops along the street
    Behind the Priests and Ruling Classes,
And fills the air where birds sang sweet
    With vestry cackle, as it passes !

Ah for the days when I was young,
When men were free and songs were sung
In old Bohemia's sylvan tongue !

Ah, for Bohemia long since fled,—
The blue sky shining overhead,
Men comrades all, all women fair,
And Freedom radiant everywhere !
Ah, then the Poet knew indeed
A tenderer soul, a softer creed,
And saw in every fair one's eyes
The light of opening Paradise ;
Then, as to lovely forms of fable
    Old poets yielded genuflection,
He knelt to Woman, all unable
To throw her corpse upon a table
    For calm aesthetical dissection !
Zola, de Goncourt, and the rest,
    Had not yet woven their witch's spell,
Not yet had Art become a pest
    To poison Love's pellucid well !
We deem'd our mistresses divine,
We pledged them deep in Shakespeare's wine,
And in the poorest robes could find
A Juliet or a Rosalind !
And when at night beneath the gas
We saw our painted sisters pass,
We hush'd our hearts like Christian men
Remembering the Magdalen !
Well, now that youth no more is mine,
I worship still the Shape Divine,
And to the outcast I am ready

To lift my hat, as to a lady ;
But when I hear the modern cry,
  Mocking the human form and face,
And watch the cynic's sensual eye,
  Blind as his little soul is base,
And see the foul miasma creep
  Destroying all things sweet and fair,
What wonder if I sometimes weep
  And feel the canker of despair ?

That mood, thank God, is evanescent,
  For I'm an optimist at heart,
And 'spite the dark and troubled Present
  See lights that stir the clouds apart !
Rare as the dodo, that strange fowl,
  (Now quite extinct thro' persecution),
Despite the hooting of the owl
  I still preserve my youth's illusion,
Believe in God and Heaven and Love,
  And turning from Life's sorry sight,
Watch starry lattices above
  Opening upon the waves of Night,—
Find shapes divine and ever fair
Thronging with radiant faces there,
While hands of benediction wave
O'er these wild waters of the grave.

Et ego in Bohemiâ fui !
Have known its fountains deep and dewy,

Have wander'd where the sun shone mellow
On many an honest ragged fellow,
And for Bohemia's sake since then
Have loved poor brothers of the pen.
I've popt at vultures circling skyward,
I've made the carrion-hawks a bye-word,
But never caused a sigh or sob in
The heart of mavis or cock-robin,
Nay, many such (let Time attest me !)
Have fed out of my hand, and blest me !
So when my wayward life is ended,
With all my sins that can't be mended,
And in my singing rags I lie
Face upward to the cruel sky,
The small birds, fluttering about me,
While birds of prey and ravens flout me,
May strew a few loose leaves above
The Outcast whom so few could love,—
And on my grave in flower-wrought words
    The Inscription set, that men may view it,—
' He blest the nameless singing birds,
Loved the Good Shepherd's flocks and herds,
    Et ille in Bohemiâ fuit ! '

EPILOGUE.

FIDES AMANTIS.

FIDES AMANTIS.

Dearest and Best ! Light of my way !
  Soul of my Soul, whom God hath sent
To be my guardian night and day,
To make me humbly kneel and pray,
  When proudest and most turbulent !
Calm of my Life ! dear Angel mine !
  Come to me, now I faint and fail,
And guide me softly to the Shrine,
Where thro' the deep'ning gloom doth shine
  Life's bleeding Heart, Love's Holy Grail,
Where Soul feels Soul, and Instinct, stirred
  To Insight, looks Creation thro',
And hear me murmur, word by word,
  The Creed I owe to Heaven and *you !*

" I do believe in God ; that He
Made Heaven and Earth, and you and me !
Nay, I believe in all the host
  Of Gods, from Jesus down to Joss,
But honour best and reverence most
  That guileless God who bore the Cross.
I do believe that this dark scheme,
  This riddle of our life below,
Is solved by Insight and by Dream,
  And not by aught mere Sense can know ;
That the one sacrifice whereby
We attest a faith which cannot die,
Is the burnt offering we place
  On Truth's pure Altar day by day,

Whereby the sensual and the base
　Within us is consumed away ;
That just as far as we forego
　Our selfish claim to stand *alone*,
Proving our gladness or our woe
　Is Humankind's and not our own,
So far as for another's sake
　Our cup of sorrow we accept,
And crave, although our hearts should break,
　The pain supreme of God's Adept,
So far shall we attain the height
Of Freedom, in the Master's sight.
I do believe that our salvation
　Lies in the little things of life,
Not in the pomp and acclamation
　Of triumph, or in battle-strife,
Not on the thrones where men are crown'd,
　Not in the race where chariots roll,
But in the arms that clasp us round
　And hold us *backward* from the goal !
In Love, not Pride ; in stooping low,
　Not soaring blindly at the sun ;
In power to feel, not zeal to know ;
　Not in rewards, but duties done.

" *Corollary* : all gain is base,
　The Victor's wreath, the Poet's crown,
If conquest in the giddy race
　Means one poor struggler trampled down,
If he who gains the sunless throne
Of Fame, sits silent and alone,
Without Humanity to share
His happiness, or his despair !

" This Gospel I uphold, the one
The latter Adam comes to prove :

To every Soul beneath the sun
  Wide open lies a Heaven of Love ;
But none, however free from sin,
  However cloth'd in pomp and pride,
However fair, may enter in,
  Without some Witness at his side,
To attest before the Judge and King
Vicarious love and suffering.
Who stands alone, shall surely fall !
  Who folds the falling to his breast
Stands sure and firm in spite of all,
  While angel-choirs proclaim him blest."

Dearest and Best ! Soul of my Soul !
  Life of my Life, kneel here with me !
Pray while the Storms around us roll,
  That God may keep us frail, yet free !
Be Love our strength ! be God our goal !
  Amen, et Benedicite !

LETTER DEDICATORY

TO

C. W. S.

A LETTER DEDICATORY TO C. W. S., IN
WESTERN AMERICA.

DEAR FRIEND,—Though I have never shaken your hand, or looked into your eyes, I know you well and love in you one of the brightest spirits of the time, a true Soul-fellow whom sooner or later, in this world or another, I am sure to meet. I knew you first when, among the sunless Hebrides, I read your beautiful descriptions of solitudes far away. Then your letters came, with their royal greeting as of king to king, and brought further hostages of your intellectual sovereignty.

What you have told me of yourself, of your dreams and sorrows, of your struggles and adventures, of the world's indifference to you and your indifference to the world, is only fresh corroboration of the goodness and wisdom I discovered in your writings,—fresh bright spirits of personality well worthy of the land of Whitman and Thoreau. You ask me to respond with particulars concerning *myself.* I cheerfully do so, though in the little I have to tell you will find only an adumbration of your own experience. You are lonely in the great solitude. I am lonelier still in the great world. We both preserve our illusions,—both are children in a period when men grow prematurely old. But you have been spared persecution, misunderstanding, misconception. You have had your share of the lotus. My life has been a weary fight for bread.

I began with high hopes and noble dreams. At nineteen years of age, after having been educated in independence, I was tost out on the stormy sea of Literature, where I have been busy ever since, beating this way and that, often almost sunk by authorized gunboats or piratical dhows, and never finding a fair wind to waft me to the Fortunate Isles. I have since had the usual experience of original men,—my worst work has been received with more or less toleration, and my best work misunderstood or neglected ; while the self-authorized critical Pilots, who haunt the shallows of journalism, have agreed that I am a factious and opinionated Mariner, doomed like my own Dutchman to eternal damnation, because like my prototype I have once or twice been provoked to violent language. For nearly a generation I have suffered a constant literary persecution. Even the good Samaritans have passed me by. Yet I survive as you know, and may even call myself contented, hating no man, fearing no man, envying no man. Few men, however, have had to struggle harder even for the merest food and air.

I am now, at the half-way House of Life, as great a simpleton in the ways of the world as ever. I do not even know if I have failed or succeeded, nor indeed do I care ; I only know that some of my failures are pleasanter to remember than what some men call my "successes." I have sought only one thing in life,—the solution of its Divine meaning ; and sometimes I think I have found it. But in an age when the gigman assures us there are no Gods, and in the strength of that assurance becomes a minister of a God-respecting cabinet, when to believe in anything but hand-to-mouth Science and dish-and-all-swallowing Politics is a sign of intellectual decrepitude, when a man cannot start better than by believing that all Humanity's previous starts have been blunders, I would rather go back to De Balsac and swear by Godhead and the Monarchy, than drift about with nothing to swear by at all. And absolutely, I don't know whether there are Gods or not. I know only that there is Love, and lofty Hope, and Divine Compassion, and that if these are delusions, you and I and all of us are no better than infusoria. If *this* is the only life I am to live, the Devil help me !—for if the Gods cannot, the Devil *must*.

You inquire, with very natural curiosity, about the leading *littérateurs* of England. My knowledge of them is of the slightest, and I know only a few who appear to take life in earnest. Our literature has run to seed in journalism. Our poets are respectable gentlemen, who have a holy horror of martyrdom. Our novels are written for young ladies' seminaries ; our men of science are fashionable physicians, printing their feeble philosophical prescriptions in the Reviews, and taking large fees for showing the poor patient, Man, that his disease is incurable. Even Herbert Spencer has sometimes drifted into this sort of empiricism. You would find London, if you ever came to it, about the most foolish place in the Universe, and furthermore, a Pandemonium of printers' devils. For myself, I have found infinitely more wisdom in Paisley or Kilmarnock. I know no sight sadder than a successful literary man, except perhaps a successful painter or musician. A very little prosperity can turn a fine human soul into a mere machine for reading and writing, eating and drinking. Often, when I feel this danger, I wish to God I had never been taught to write and read.

You must not gather from this that I am in revolt against my fellow-workers ; on the contrary, I love the inky fellows immensely, when they are not spoiled by prosperity. And frankly, I myself have not escaped the charge of selling my birthright for a mess of pottage ; of gaining my bread by hodman's labour, when I might have been sitting empty-stomached on Parnassus. Yes, I of all men ; I who after ten years of solitude should have gone mad if I had not rushed back into the thick of life, yet who, even there, have been haunted by the ghosts of the solitude left behind, and have never bowed my head to any idol or cared for any recompense but the love of men. My errors, however, have arisen from excess of human sympathy, from ardour of human activity, rather than from any great love for the loaves and fishes. Lacking the pride of intellect, I have by superabundant activity tried to prove myself a man among men, not a mere *littérateur*. Moreover, I have never yet discovered in myself, or in any man, any gift which entitles me to despise the meanest of my fellows. So I have stooped to hodman's work occasionally, mainly because I cannot pose in the godlike manner of your lotus-eaters. I have not humoured my reputation. I have thought no work undignified which did not convert me into a Specialist or a Prig. I have written for all men and in all moods. But the birthright which belongs to all Poets has never been offered by me in any market, and my manhood has never been stained by any sham hate or sham affection.

N

With all this, I have for nearly a quarter of a century been beating the air. I have been thinking of the Gods, in days when the Temples of the Gods are roofless and untenanted ; I have been yearning to the Heavens, which are empty above me ; I have been crying to God for a sign, and the only sign I have seen is the universal Cross of Sorrow. With a heart overflowing with love, I have gathered to myself only hate and misconception,—and all this for one reason only, that I have endeavoured to avoid self-worship, and to find some slight foothold of human truth.

I have been reproached, bitterly reproached, for writing stage plays ; for I may tell you that there is a superstition here, among our literary cicerones, that the Drama is in a bad way. You, however, will understand me when I say that play-writing has been to me a source of very great help and happiness ; that it has taken me from the solitudes where I nearly died, and cured me, by its practical necessities, of much literary egotism. I was not brought up to carpentering or any honest trade, so I learned, as far as my powers would allow me, the trade of play-writing. Even my enemies admit that I have some coarse skill in that way, and *au reste*, it has brought me bread. Do not conceive from these words that I despise the craft. It is a good and fitting one, bracing to an intellect too much given to dreaming and introspection, and it has thrown me into close collision with my fellow-men. I have always loved the stage and players : simple folk, these, grown-up children, babbling of Bohemia and green fields, of Bardolph and the tavern. Yet even here, as I have said, I have given much offence,—for the literary Prig of this generation despises the thinker who is not a dullard, a prosaist, and a hypocrite. Knowing this, some of the craftsmen and journeymen around me take themselves and their craft very seriously, write art with a capital " A,' and so befool the foolish ones.

Which brings me, by the way, to a subject of deep personal interest to all who, like yourself, look upon this Babylon with eyes of envy. Elsewhere, in a book which I shall shortly send you,* I have touched in plain prose on certain curious phenomena of the Hour,—among others, on beneficent legislation and political trades-

* " The Coming Terror, and other Essays."

union. For some years past, moreover, a solemn league and cove-
nant has been entered into by journalists, to coerce, intimidate, and
silence all non-union men,—*id est*, all men who revolt against the
hideous multiplicity of Cockney scandal, literary tittle-tattle,
Podsnapian criticism, and noisy playing on the French horn.
When in America, I noticed in your newspapers a curious pheno-
menon,—a secret hatred and suspicion of all original men who, by
genius or fortune, had risen from the ranks, and the want of
reverence reached its acme when some of your newspapers
printed woodcuts, reproduced by photography, of the *cancer-cells*
then destroying the life of a great man who "had done the State
some service "—General Grant. Here the same feeling is rapidly
spreading. Every man who writes a book, or who becomes otherwise prominent, is under newspaper espionage. Swarms of busy
bodies live on him, follow him, and even when they praise, insult
him. He is the prey of a plague of hornets. If he resents the
persecution, the whole trades-union of journalism is down upon
him. By only one thing is he saved,—the multiplicity of his an-
tagonists, who destroy each other. Woe to him if he speaks his
true mind on any subject! Woe to him if he believes in anything
beyond the common judgment of the hour!

As I write these lines, they are bringing over the body of a
great Poet (whom I knew well in the flesh) to bury it in Westminster Abbey,—a sacred place, I may explain, where we place a
few of our master-thinkers among hecatombs of mediocrities.
Robert Browning is to lie, to his and our glory, by the side of
that estimable and once prosperous versifier, Abraham Cowley.
The life of the modern Poet was darkened by constant neglect and
infinite detraction. If it had not been for the efforts of a small
body of devoted worshippers, who preached Browningese in spite
of endless ridicule, he would scarcely have been heard of by the
great public. Again and again, when he was issuing his works of
thought and imagination, he was informed that it was a Poet's
duty not to instruct, but to amuse, his generation. A leading
critical authority compared him to a noisy and mannered "Auc-
tioneer." He was requested to favour the world with light per-
formances, suitable for the suburban reciter and drawing-room

entertainer. Since he was an eager man among men, *en rapport*
with everything human, he was described as a worldling and a
diner-out. Suddenly, on his death, the newspapers discovered
that he was a sublime person, a great person. Column upon
column was written in his praise by gentlemen who had scarcely
read one of his works. "He was great," was the cry ; "bury him
at Westminster." And scarcely was he cold when it was deeply
regretted that he missed wearing the Laurel, still worn, we poets
thank God, by the Galahad of modern Poesy. How many re-
flected that in this last case, for a miracle, it was the Poet who
dignified the Laurel, not the Laurel which dignified the Poet. That
same Laurel had been worn, and will be worn again, by triumphant
mediocrity. It is for the moment a sacred thing, because two true
Poets have condescended to it, but in all sane men's eyes it is in
itself a shabby and a barren honour, a dreary and discredited
inheritance.

The World, which now and again in fits of *post mortem* enthu-
siasm professes to respect Poets, insults them daily and hourly by
shameful comparisons. This Poet is greater than that, forsooth,
and that Poet sings more prettily than this. For not even yet
does the world know what a Poet *is*, as distinguished from a poet-
laureate or a poetaster. Between Poets there can be no comparisons,
because all are equal by right of birth and equality of vision.
Among *them*, the Seers of humanity, there is neither rank nor
competition. The only honour they seek is the love and sympathy
of the few who understand them, and to whom they minister in
secret joy.

Forgetful also of what Poetry itself is, we have from generation
to generation suffered the rankest weeds to grow upon Parnassus.
Two-thirds of our native poetic growth from Euphues downwards
is mere verbiage, and of late years verbiage has blossomed with
the amazing splendour of a sun-flower. Hence it is that, to nine-
tenths of the few people who read Verse at all, the Poet is a
voluble person with nothing to say, who charms the ear with
popular tunes, in the manner of Mrs Shaw the whistling lady.
It is particularly stipulated that a Poet must on no account be
tedious in the sense of possessing any ideas, and if such ideas as

he does possess are not in harmony with the social *status quo*, woe
to him! Otherwise, a Singer's success is estimated by the number
of foolish people who quote his catch lines and whistle his tunes.
But the change is at hand. I have waited twenty years for it to
come, but it comes at last. Poetry, which alone has resisted the
genius of the age, which has continued retrograde while all other
Arts advanced, will move to its due place among those agencies
which influence the Life of Man. It will not leave the prose
romancist and the story-teller to deal with the facts of existence.
It will forget the tales of Troy and Eden, and sing the pity of
Humanity instead of the wrath of Achilles.

Pray do not misunderstand me. I am not echoing the cry,
heard now in Europe from Moscow to Paris, from Paris to London,
that Literature must be only an "indecent photograph" of Life.
I am not approving that banal Fiction and Drama which deals
only with the stomach-aches, the stranguries, and the ovarian
ailments of unhealthy types of humanity. An exhausted breed of
men and women has produced an exhausted Literature, and the
Anæmic Book faces us everywhere. Therein, however, is not Life,
but Death. In England as elsewhere, impotent writers, hating the
very thought of Health and Humour, have been *poisoning the Wells*.
What literature wants now is not more prurient self-analysis, but
less. How another Rabelais, another Fielding, another Byron,
might refresh the world! Sheer rampant animalism, comic
devilry, coarseness of speech and phrase, would be better far than
the intellectual self-pollution which is now so fashionable. Better
to *do* something Titanic in even wickedness, than to remain
miserable half-born creatures, analysing our own nasty little sensa-
tions, and thinking *them* Titanic! Why all this "pother" about
our moral secretions? Why all this fear of honest natural
functions? Why all this fumbling and fibbing between the sexes?
Is it because we have lost the Gods, and having nothing to gaze
up to, must fain feast our downcast eyes on the centre umbilical,
whence radiate all these foul ecstasies and visions? O for one
glimpse of honest Adam and Eve, naked but unashamed! O for
one large breath of Gargantua,—nay, even for one rash witticism
of Panurge!

But I am digressing into criticism, when my purpose was merely a personal explanation. I have said enough, however, to shew you that the barren honour of popularity is not for me, and though I do not contend for a moment that to be unpopular is a personal merit, it is certain that freedom of poetic thought is seldom compatible with literary comfort. If I were to find a fault with some of the really fine and prosperous Poets of our period, it would be this—that their prosperity has resulted less from their totality of merit than through their sympathy with the social and political environment. For example, it is to me individually an inconceivable thing that any Poet should approve the contemporary standards of Christianity, or write political pæans in favour of the most monstrous of human accomplishments, that of War. It is equally inconceivable to me that any Poet should desert even the worship of Priapus for that of St Jingo, or hail with rapture the existence of institutions which are based on hereditary wrong-doing, and on the sacrifice of our nation or class of human beings to another class or nation. A Poet, to my thinking, is a Prophet and a Propagandist, or nothing; and to be a Propagandist or a Poet, is to be cursed in the market place, not crowned in the forum. Fortunately, the best of our singers have been so cursed, not so crowned. But there must be some strange confusion of thought, or some insincerity of expression, in a writer who, like Carlyle, " writes God large " all over his books, and at the same time tells his Boswell that " God does nothing "—in other words, that there is no God at all. I well remember the amazement and concern of the late Mr Browning when I informed him, on one occasion, that he was an advocate of Christian Theology, nay an essentially Christian teacher and preacher. In the very face of Mr Browning's masterly books, which certainly support the opinion then advanced, I hereby affirm and attest that the writer regarded that expression of opinion as an impeachment and a slight. I therefore put the question categorically, " Are you not, then, a Christian ? " He immediately thundered, " *No !* "

Which brings me by natural transition to the last point of controversy in which I shall touch in this letter. The insincerity of modern society, the desire for compromise, in matters of religion, has penetrated even to the Thinkers. Perhaps, of all living publicists, the only one who has uttered his thought openly and fearlessly is Mr Bradlaugh, the politician. I do not sympathise with that thought, and I am glad to suspect that maturity has modified it very considerably, but it was honest thought, expressed in a vocabulary that could not be mistaken. Among poets the late James Thomson, a belated and unfortunate singer, and the late Richard Jefferies, a poet in prose, suffered cruel neglect and persecution for a similar kind of honesty. Better, surely, such sincerity than any compromise, however expedient. For a Poet to join the herd of hollow hearts, the mob of publicists and politicians, who worship in the shrines they believe to be empty of all godhead, is a thing too horrible for contemplation.

I, for my part, who was nourished on the husks of Socialism and the chill water of Infidelity, who was born in Robert Owen's New Moral World, and who scarcely heard even the name of God till at ten years of age I went to godly Scotland, have been God-intoxicated ever since I first saw the Mountains and the Sea. Without the sanction of the Supernatural, the certainty of the Superhuman, Life to me is nothing. Yet do I not know, am I not told on every hand, that all the Gods are dead, and is it not certain that the last Poets are following the last Gods? Science is paralysing literature, and the specialists of Pessimism are verifying Schopenhauer in the dissecting-rooms and the lupanars. One of our judges, and a good judge too, loudly proclaims that Religion is inexpedient, and that this world, so long as it lasts, is all-sufficient. One of our scientists, eager to sustain the institutions of property, avers that Force and Theft are condoned by the lapse of years, and even necessitated by the natural inequality of men. Absolute ethics of any kind is ridiculed, not only in politics, but in all the concerns of life. Yet Herbert Spencer is speaking, to a world which will not listen. In the face of all this, we belated Poets, mad and heartbroken at the death of our ideals, are asked to strum the guitar, to "amuse" our generation.

Ah, well, it will soon be over! Happily, the puzzle of this life does not last for long. Meantime, perhaps, I have convinced you that London is only Babylon under a new name. If you ever come to it, I know you will not linger. But whether you come or come not, let us share this secret between us—that though the Gods may be dead as men say, their wraiths still haunt the earth. Even here, in this Babylon, this London, they walk nightly and fulfil their ghostly ministrations. Pan flits through the darkness of Whitechapel, under the cupola of St Paul's I have seen Apollo face to face, Aphrodite has pillowed my head upon her naked breast, and as for the weary world-worn God of Galilee, he is everywhere, still pleading for us, still wondering that his Father shuts himself away. Was not our Elder Brother out yonder on the Pacific with Father Damien, and is he not here incarnate wherever the bread of charity is broken? The last word of the Soul is not yet said. When it is uttered, in the midst of this Belshazzar's Feast of modern Culture, both Gods and Poets will live again. Meantime, they haunt the dark hours of sorrow and of insight, and whisper " Wait ! "

One last word, concerning the poem which I now send you. It is, as you will see, incomplete, but in itself comprehensible. I will wager you, however, the whole set of Chambers' English Poets to one of your far more precious letters, that this book is either universally boycotted or torn into shreds ; that its purpose is misunderstood, and that above all, it is impeached on the ground of its " morality." Yet it is a live thing, part of the very seed of my living Soul. I would read every line of it to the woman I loved, to her whose purity was most sacred to me, and I would accept her judgment upon it, knowing that she would tell me, " This book is pure, and page after page of it is written in your own blood." And so I toss it to the birds of prey, even while I dedicate it, with my love and friendship, to you, one of the few who will understand it. It is only the beginning ; the record of what every modern man has known, or *must* know. The rest will follow, I hope, in due time ; and the end, perhaps, may even justify the beginning.

ROBERT BUCHANAN.

TURNBULL AND SPEARS, PRINTERS, EDINBURGH.